• • • • • •

"Have people started asking about us?"

She pursed her lips. "A little."

"What are they saying?"

"Just being nosey. They wanted to know why I visited you on the other floors."

"What'd you tell them?"

"I told them I've been your nurse for eight years, and there's nothing wrong with me wanting to check on you and see how you're doing."

"Am I getting you in trouble?" he wondered.

"Evan, don't worry about the gossips here. No one in this hospital is going to keep me from checking on you. If I have to see you on another floor or come in on my day off... Whatever it takes, I'll always be here for you."

Evan's heart fluttered. Surely she knew her words gave him life. His heart thudded as he considered his next question. He feared the life she had just given him could be taken away just as quickly.

"Jada, is it common for a patient to fall in love with his nurse?"

Her throat caught. He watched her eyes dilate. Her eyelids fluttered before she responded.

"Um, no, Evan. It's not common, but it does happen. When people are scared and vulnerable, they appreciate the people they believe are saving them. Sometimes that appreciation manifests as affection. It's called the Florence Nightingale effect."

"Why do they call it that?"

Her breaths came in shudders. "I don't, I don't know."

"Is it common for a nurse to fall in love with a patient?" he asked.

She shook her head. "No. That's not common."

"Has it ever happened to you? Have you ever fallen in love with a patient?"

She continued to shake her head as she rose from her seat. Her legs were unsteady. She prayed he wouldn't notice. "No, Evan. I haven't. I – I'm sorry."

She left the room without another word.

• • • • • •

EVAN'S HEART

EVAN'S HEART

KEITH THOMAS WALKER

KEITHWALKERBOOKS, INC
This is a UMS production

KEITHWALKERBOOKS

Publishing Company
KeithWalkerBooks, Inc.
P.O. Box 690
Allen, TX 75013

For information write
KeithWalkerBooks, Inc.
P.O. Box 690
Allen, TX 75013

ISBN-13 DIGIT: 978-1-7320624-8-1
ISBN-10 DIGIT: 1-7320624-8-X
Library of Congress Control Number: 2020936607
Manufactured in the United States of America

Second Edition

Visit us at www.keithwalkerbooks.com

5

This book is for my rose gold Queen

MORE BOOKS BY
KEITH THOMAS WALKER

How to Kill Your Husband
A Good Dude
Riding the Corporate Ladder
The Finley Sisters' Oath of Romance
Blow by Blow
Jewell and the Dapper Dan
Harlot
Plan C (And More KWB Shorts)
Dripping Chocolate
The Realest Ever
Jackson Memorial
Sleeping With the Strangler
Life After
Blood for Isaiah
Brick House
Brick House 2
One on One
Brick House 3
Jackson Memorial 2
Backslide
Threesome
Backslide 2
Threesome 2
Election Day

NOVELLAS

Might be Bi Part One
Harder
Primal Part One

The Realest Christmas Ever
Hotline Fling

POETRY COLLECTION

Poor Righteous Poet

FINLEY HIGH SERIES

Prom Night at Finley High
Fast Girls at Finley High
Bullies at Finley High

Visit keithwalkerbooks.com for information about these and upcoming titles from KeithWalkerBooks

ACKNOWLEDGMENTS

Of course I would like to thank God, first and foremost, for giving me the creativity and drive to pursue my dreams and the understanding that I am nothing without Him. I would like to thank my beautiful wife and my mother for always pushing me to be the best I can be. I would like to thank Janae Hafford for being the best advisor, supporter and little sister a brother could ever have.

I would also like to thank (in no particular order) Beulah Neveu, Deloris Harper, Denise Fizer, Michele Halsey Hallahan, Priscilla C. Johnson, Kim Tanner, Tia Kelly, Edwina Putney, Melissa Carter, Cathy Atchison, Lanita Irvin, Ramona Weathersbee, Cynthia Antoinette Taylor, Jason Owens, Ramona Brown, Johnathan Royal, Sharon Blount, BRAB Book Club, and Uncle Steven Thomas, one love. I'd like to thank everyone who purchased and enjoyed one of my books. Everything I do has always been to please you. I know there are folks who mean the world to me that I'm failing to mention. I apologize ahead of time. Rest assured I'm grateful for everything you've done for me!

CHAPTER ONE
FAMILIAR PLACES

"He's getting paid and laid. It must be the shades."

Evan stood next to Jeremy's desk grinning broadly.

"No way," his young coworker said, a smile gradually broadening on his face.

"Yep," Evan touted.

"You cleared it with Melissa?"

"Of course I did."

Melissa was the marketing manager at Ray-Ban. Evan's company, T9 Solutions, was ultimately responsible for producing the ad, but Melissa would have to approve the final product.

"I mean, I know this is going in Playboy, but..."

"But what?" Evan asked. At six-foot two, 220 pounds, he towered over his colleague, even when Jeremy wasn't seated. He wore a full beard with a trimmed moustache. His skin tone was medium brown. "You don't think it's sexy?"

"Oh, it's plenty sexy," Jeremy said, returning his attention to his monitor. "If you say it's a go, it's a go." He quickly typed the tagline and positioned it mid-right of the models.

Evan walked around his desk and looked over his shoulder. "Wait, what happened to the other models?"

"I thought we were going with this guy?"

"I like him," Evan said, staring at the smartly dressed man sporting the Ray-Ban product. His eyes narrowed. "But it won't work for this tagline. You had the one with a woman and man, the guy with the slim-fit suit..."

"Oh, yeah, I still have it."

Jeremy did his magic, and the new image replaced the first.

"Yeah, that's him," Evan said, scrutinizing the photo. "I like that. He definitely looks like he's getting paid."

"And from the look in her eyes," Jeremy said, referring to the female model, "I'd say he's getting laid."

"It must be the shades!" they both said and laughed.

The male model sported a pair of sleek Ray-Ban's. He was young, cool and confident. He was a mover and a shaker. He didn't look like he ever stressed about a mortgage payment or a relationship. Even the woman devouring him with her eyes barely caught his attention.

"This is a winner," Jeremy declared as he positioned the rest of the printed information on the ad.

"Yeah," Evan agreed. "But I need that tagline to *pop*. Why don't you–"

"I got you," Jeremy said as he adjusted the font, color and size. "How about this?"

"Shift the–"

"Got it."

Evan chuckled inwardly as his coworker made the adjustment. After working together for fifteen years, he would swear Jeremy could read his mind. Sure enough, he shifted the last line, "Must be the shades," in the direction Evan was going to suggest.

"Okay, what do you think?"

Evan patted him on the shoulder. "My man. Send it to me," he said as he stepped away from his desk. "I wanna run it by Gwen before we tinker with the graphics."

"Sent," Jeremy said before he was twenty paces away.

Evan accessed the file on his iPad and headed for his manager's office.

Working as a content marketer wasn't on his radar when he majored in journalism 24 years ago. Back then, Evan envisioned himself winning the Pulitzer prize for a hard-hitting Exxon exposé. Or maybe he'd find himself reporting from the frontline of whatever war-torn Muslim country the United States decided to attack by the time he graduated college. But life has a way of taking you in different directions. As far as divergent paths go, he was happy with the way things had turned out.

Gwen was manager of their print ad division. Since he'd been with the company, Evan had the pleasure to shine in all departments: print, digital, television and radio. He didn't have a preference, when it came to the work, but he always enjoyed working with Gwen. Although she was only ten years his senior, she gave off motherly vibes that made him long for his family in Washington. She had smooth, dark skin, a slim figure and serious eyes that were known to be extremely critical of the work her department produced.

"Morning," Evan said as he stepped into her office. "How was your weekend?"

"It was a weekend," she replied without rising from her seat.

"You can't refer to a weekend with the same dryness you'd refer to a Monday."

"I kept the grandkids Friday night, took them to dance and karate practice Saturday morning, dropped them off, caught a movie with Richard, dinner at Cheddar's and worked all day Sunday," she informed him.

Evan chuckled. "You make your family time sound like a chore, but I know you loved every minute of it."

Her smile was subtle but not lost on him. "What about you?" she asked. "Did you get anything done this weekend?"

"Not on the business side, but I got right to work when I got here today. Check it out," he said, offering her his iPad.

Her smile was unmistakable this time.

"Did you clear that tagline with Melissa?"

"Of course I did."

"Who came up with it?" Her eyes continued to study the ad.

"You think anyone in this building *besides me* can come up with something this brilliant?"

"So modest you are."

"You know I'm kidding."

"It's okay," she said. "You've got a right to be proud of this. You do amazing work. I love it."

"Thank you."

"You and Jeremy put this together?"

"Yes. We have a little more work to do on the graphics. Wanted to get your opinion before we finalize it."

"You and Jeremy should go into business together. Every time you... Evan?"

From her perspective, her esteemed colleague's eyes fluttered as he swayed briefly before falling quickly to the floor, like a toy robot that had its battery pack unexpectedly removed.

From Evan's perspective, there was a slight tightening in his chest before the world swam in dark gray and black dots, and he felt himself sliding down a dark tube. The experience was oddly comforting. He didn't have the wherewithal to reach out and try to break his fall before he impacted the thin carpet.

He awakened in the back of an ambulance. Two EMT's were busy affixing telemetry pads and leads to strategic areas of his torso. His shirt had been removed. He lie flat on a stretcher, part of his vision obscured by an oxygen mask affixed to his face.

He sat up unexpectedly. His brain rewarded him with a sensation of vertigo. He squeezed his eyes closed to ward off the dizziness.

"Whoa there," the man on his right said.

"Evan, you need to lie back down," the woman on his left advised him. She placed a hand on his chest and prodded him in that direction.

Evan didn't fight against her, but he braced himself up with an elbow and maintained his position. When he opened his eyes again, he saw the back of the ambulance was open.

Gwen stood in the parking lot, her expression as worried as he would expect. Jeremy stood a step behind her.

"Evan, could you please lie back?" the female EMT said again.

"Wait a second," he protested. "I just woke up in the back of an ambulance. Is it okay if I ask some questions?"

He thought his voice sounded muffled behind the oxygen mask, but the paramedics seemed to understand him perfectly. They removed his mask.

"What happened?" Evan asked.

Gwen stepped forward. "You passed out in my office. You weren't out that long. The ambulance showed up less than five minutes ago."

"I'm alright," Evan said to the male EMT. "I think I'll be fine. I don't need to go to the hospital."

"Do you have a history of heart problems?" the paramedic asked.

That question was too specific. By then Evan's head had cleared enough to fix a look of *How could you?* on his manager. Gwen pursed her lips and actually rolled her neck slightly, as if to say, *So what if I did?*

"Yes," Evan grudgingly told the EMT. "CHF."

"Then you definitely need to let us take you to the hospital," the EMT said.

"Can't I take myself there?" he asked. "Or Jeremy – he can take me."

His coworker nodded in agreement. "I can take him, if that's okay with you two."

"It would be best if we make sure you're stable first," the female paramedic countered. "We can do that now, but in the time that will take, we would've made it halfway to the hospital. It's best if we take you, just in case."

"Yeah, but–"

"Hush you," Gwen said. "You need to let these people do their job. Scared me half to death when you fell out. I'm still shaking. I don't know if you're being macho or fool-headed right now, but these people are here to help, and you're gonna let them. Now lie back and let them do their job."

Evan sighed in resignation. The problem with having a boss who gave off motherly vibes was sometimes she took the role too seriously.

"Can I, can I at least call my wife first?" he asked the paramedics.

One of them retrieved his phone.

He cringed as he unlocked it and phoned Delores. Fortunately, the call went to voicemail.

"Hey, baby. I'm, uh, I'm headed to the hospital. I think I passed out at work, and they called an ambulance. I'm okay, but they insist on taking me to the ER. I'll, uh, I'll call you when I get there."

He sighed again and returned his phone to the EMT. He continued to plead to his manager with his eyes as they affixed his oxygen mask. Her expression remained resolute, but he saw fear and concern too. He hated himself for making her worry about him.

He lie back, and the paramedics resumed applying stickers to his skin. A monitor mounted on an IV pole awaited the heart rhythm the electrodes would provide.

Jackson Memorial was not a pleasant sight, but it was a familiar one. After being denied the request to exit the ambulance on his own two feet or at least be wheeled into the ER by wheelchair, Evan relented to his caregivers and allowed the process to play out as they wished.

He remained in the ER long enough for his nurse to declare him stable and for his cardiologist to arrive at the hospital. Dr. Davi initially diagnosed him with congestive heart failure eight years ago. Evan hoped his fainting spell was insignificant enough to warrant an immediate discharge. Dr. Davi approached his stretcher with a smile, but she did not deliver the news he expected.

"How are you Evan?" She was a slight woman in her late fifties. Her middle eastern accent was mild.

"I feel fine," he said. "I fainted or passed out at work. Not sure what that was about."

She didn't respond as she assessed his rhythm on the EKG monitor mounted above his bed. She removed the stethoscope from around her neck and plugged the earpieces in her ears.

"Could you take a deep breath?" she asked as she placed the chest-piece near his heart.

Evan complied. She repositioned the chest-piece and continued to listen. Her smile returned as she returned the stethoscope to its perch around her neck.

"I'm sending you to the cardiac tower for monitoring."

Evan rolled his eyes. "Is that really necessary?"

"I don't anticipate keeping you overnight. I know how you feel about being here."

But how could she truly know? At 42, Evan understood he was past the prime of his life, but he didn't feel like he was over the hill – at least he didn't want to feel that way. He certainly didn't want to have the word *terminal* hanging over him, but every trip to the hospital seemed to propel him towards that destiny.

Jackson Memorial had three floors in the "heart tower." Cardiac ICU, on the first floor, was for those critically ill. Cardiovascular ICU on the 2nd floor housed heart surgery patients. The third and fourth floors were cardiac telemetry. Evan was sent to C3 on most of his visits, as he was on this date. His wife called a few minutes after a PCT got him settled in.

"Hey, baby."

"Evan, what's wrong? Are you alright?" The dread in her voice made him feel worse than he already did.

"Yes, baby. I'm fine. I fainted at work, or something like that, and they called 9-1-1."

"Where are you? They took you to the hospital?"

"Yeah, I'm back on C3. Dr. Davi wants to observe me for a while, but she says she doesn't plan to keep me overnight."

"Okay. I'm sorry I'm just now getting your message. I was in a meeting, and I had my phone on silent. We have a couple of hours left in school, and I was supposed to stay to meet with the attendance committee. Do you need me there? Do you think you can handle this on your own?"

Evan understood that his wife's duties as an assistant principal made it difficult for her to take calls in the middle of the day.

"It's okay," he told her. "Don't leave work. Everything's fine. If you're still working when I get off, I can get a ride to my office and get my car."

"Get a ride? From who? You don't want me to come?"

"It's not that. I just, I feel bad enough about what happened. I passed out right in front of my boss, freaked her out. I don't need anyone else's day to get disrupted by this."

"*Disrupted*? It's not like you're calling me to bring you a spare key because you lost yours. You're in the hospital. This is serious."

"It's not serious every time I come to the hospital. Sometimes it is, and you're aware of those times. Today it's not. If I'm still here when you're done with your meeting, you can head this way. But I'm sure I'll be discharged by then."

After a pause, she sighed. "Okay, Evan. If that's what you want."

He wasn't sure if she really wanted to come, or if she was eager for him to give him an out. He told her, "I'll be okay."

"You'll call me as soon as they give you an update?"

"Yes, I promise. Get back to work. Don't worry. I'm fine."

"Alright. I'm gonna call Sharelle. If she's done with classes for the day–"

"Don't call Sharelle. She worries about me more than you do."

"Evan."

"Delores, could you let me come to the hospital this one time without getting everyone all worked up? Just this one time."

"Alright, but you know you're being stubborn."

"Fine, call me stubborn. Don't call Sharelle."

Sharelle walked into his room an hour later, while his PCT was taking his vitals.

"Daddy, what's this I hear about you not wanting anyone to know you're in the hospital."

"Yet, here you are."

He couldn't help but smile at her. Sharelle took after her father in many ways, from her height to her skin complexion and full lips. Always athletic, she was a business major at Texas Lutheran, awarded a full ride with a basketball scholarship. She approached the bed with large, wet eyes. It broke Evan's heart to know she'd been crying.

"Mama said you passed out at work."

"I did, honey, but I'm okay now. It's nothing."

"Well, what happened then? Why would you pass out, if it's nothing? What's going on with him?" she asked the PCT. "What did the doctor say?"

Caught off guard by the new energy in the room, the PCT's eyes and mouth widened at the same time.

"I – I don't have any information about him. Do you want me to get his nurse in here?"

Evan said, "No."

Sharelle said, "Yes," at the same time.

"I'm waiting on Dr. Davi," Evan told his daughter. "She's gonna give me an update and let me get out of here soon. If you want to wait, you can hear what she has to say for yourself."

"I'm not going anywhere," she assured him.

They remained silent until the PCT got her numbers and exited the room. Sharelle confronted him the moment they were alone.

"Daddy, why didn't you call me? Why do you want to be at the hospital by yourself?"

"I don't want to be here at all," he complained. "But if I have to be here, I don't need everyone in my life disrupting their schedule to come."

"Mama told me you said that. What do you, you think you're some kind of burden to us?"

"I, I think over time it can be a burden," he acknowledged. "Yes, I do feel that way."

"Well, you're not."

"How many times have you been at this hospital, on this floor or the ER or ICU?"

"What difference does that make? I'll come here a million times to be with you, if that's what it takes to get you better."

Evan bit his tongue to stifle his reply. What if he *wasn't* getting better?

"Okay, well you're here, so can we stop arguing about it? I'm sorry I didn't call you. I honestly thought I was doing the right thing by not getting you involved this time, but I can see that I wasn't."

She stepped closer to the bed and placed a hand on his cheek. "No, it only made me scared and hurt at the same time."

Her touch melted his heart, as did the fresh tears in her eyes.

"How do you feel?" she asked. "Tell me the truth? Does your chest hurt?"

"The only thing I feel right now is love," he said honestly. "My chest doesn't hurt at all."

Dr. Davi came thirty minutes later with her prognosis, or lack thereof. "Evan, I'm not sure what happened today. Your vitals look good. I didn't hear anything new when I listened to your heart. But passing out is not a good thing for anyone, especially a heart patient. I need to evaluate you further, before I know what steps we need to take."

Evan's heart sank. It sounded like she wanted to keep him overnight.

Fortunately, she said, "I would like to schedule an ECHO, so I can get a good look at your heart. You can do it as an outpatient."

"Great," he replied. He'd agree to a colonoscopy to get out of there.

"You can schedule it before you leave or call tomorrow. Your nurse will come and give you your discharge orders in a few minutes." She gave Sharelle a comforting smile. "How are you, angel?"

"I'm fine. Worried about my dad."

"Yes, I know how you feel. We're doing the best we can to get his heart back to one hundred percent."

"I know you are. We appreciate everything you're doing."

When they were alone in the room again, Evan told her, "Why don't you get back to school? I'm gonna stop by the job to get my car, and then I'll head home. I'll call you when I get there, to let you know I made it."

Sharelle rolled her eyes in exasperation. "Why are you doing everything you can to get me to leave you alone?"

"Because you're twenty-one, and you need to be enjoying your college experience."

"I don't know how enjoyable you think my night will be if I leave my dad in the hospital."

"I think–"

"You think too much," she told him. "Maybe that's why you're taking so long to heal, because you're too busy worrying about trying to do everything yourself."

"You are stubborn."

"When Mama called me, she said the same thing about you," she said with a smirk.

Evan couldn't help but laugh at his mini-me.

A nurse knocked on the door a minute later.

"Hey, you ready to go?"

"Yes, we are!" Sharelle said and began to gather her things.

"Been ready," Evan agreed. "Don't take nothing to get a brother up in here, but I feel like I need an act of congress to get out!"

CHAPTER TWO
FAMILY TIES

Delores called again as Evan sat in the passenger seat of his daughter's Honda. It was 3:45 pm.

He answered, "Hey baby."

"Evan, what's going on. Where are you?"

"I'm with Sharelle, on the way back to work to get my car."

"Why didn't you tell me you were being discharged. You said you'd call when you got an update."

"It wasn't much of an update. Dr. Davi doesn't know what's wrong. She wants me to come in for an ECHO. She said I could do it as an outpatient."

"When are you going to do that?"

"I haven't scheduled it yet. I'll call them tomorrow."

"How are you feeling?"

"I feel fine. I didn't feel anything strange before I passed out. I don't feel any differently now. I don't know what happened."

"Do you need me to head home? I have a meeting I'm supposed to go to, but I can head straight home, if you need me to."

"No, go ahead and go to your meeting. I should be home by the time you get there. I have something I need to check on when I get to the office."

In the driver's seat, his daughter shot him a look. His wife must have been thinking the same thing.

Delores said, "You're going back to work?"

"Just for a little bit."

"Do you think that's a good idea?"

"Says Mrs. Workakolic."

"But I'm not sick," she shot back.

"And I'm not bedridden," he said. "I'll only be in there for thirty minutes, an hour tops."

"Okay, Evan. How's Sharelle doing?"

"She's fine, but I think I'm about to get an earful, when I get off the phone."

"You..." After a pause, she said, "The ambulance ride – they said that was necessary? When you left that message earlier, you didn't sound like you were incapacitated."

"I didn't want to ride in the ambulance. I told them so. I asked if Jeremy could take me, but they weren't trying to hear it."

"It's just, those things are so expensive. The ER visit is bad enough, but the ambulance... I feel like sometimes they try to rack up the charges. That bill is gonna be a monster, and now they want another ECHO..."

Evan couldn't give the response he wanted, with his daughter sitting next to him, so he didn't respond at all.

"Well, as long as you're okay," Delores conceded. "I'll see you in a little bit."

When he got off the phone, his daughter picked up where his wife left off.

"Did you tell Mom you're going back to work? I thought you were just going to get your car."

"I just have to take care of something I was working on before I left," he told her. "It's not really *work*. It's not like I'm doing manual labor."

"Dad, you do too much. There's nothing going on in that place that can't wait."

"I promise I won't be there too long. I'll call you as soon as I get home. Actually, I'll call you when I leave, and we can talk while I drive home, if you're worried."

He didn't realize he opened a can of worms with that comment until her eyes widened.

"Are you even okay to drive home? What if you pass out again behind the wheel?"

It was a fair question, but, "The doctor didn't say anything about me not driving."

"We didn't ask. Dad, I don't think it's a good idea. You just got out of the hospital. Until they do that ECHO, I think you need to stay home and get some rest."

"Listen, baby girl. I know you want the best for me. You have to understand I'm doing the best I can to get better. If at some point that requires me to stay home in bed all day, I'll do it. But I hope it never comes to that. And the doctor didn't say that's what I needed to do. You were there. I need you to trust that I'm not going to do anything to hurt myself. I love you."

"I love you too, Daddy."

"Do you want me to call you when I leave work?"

She nodded. She continued to look fretful, but at least her eyes were dry. He reached and touch her hand, which was resting on the gearshift. She didn't look away from the

road as they interlocked fingers. They maintained the bond
for the duration of the drive.

In the office, Evan found that a good number of his
coworkers were aware of the earlier incident. Having seen
only Jeremy and Gwen through the ambulance doors, he
hoped he could slip in under the radar. But it was an hour
before quitting time, and the building was full. More than a
few dozen coworkers either gave him curious stares or
approached to ask if he was okay. Evan assured them he was
as fit as a fiddle.

"I just got a little dizzy. I'm fine."

His closest ally was the most shocked to see him back
so soon. Evan knew that was because Jeremy had seen him
in the back of the ambulance, with an oxygen mask and
electrodes snaking from his body.

When Evan approached his desk, Jeremy said, "What
are you doing here? I didn't think you'd be back today."

"Nah, I'm good." Evan took a seat next to him. "I
gotta get a test done later this week, but doc says I'm fine.
How's that Ray-Ban ad looking?"

Jeremy looked like he had a million questions, not a
single one of them about Ray-Ban's. He reluctantly tore his
eyes away from Evan's and pulled up the ad on his laptop.

"Nice," Evan said, noticing the work he'd done on the
graphics. "Now that I see this, I'm thinking we could–"

"*Evan.*"

The sharp voice made him recoil slightly. He looked up and saw Gwen marching towards him. She softened her approach when she was close enough to speak without raising her voice.

"Could you come to my office, please?"

Rather than turn and lead the way, she watched as he rose from his seat. Evan sensed she was looking for any sign of weakness or fatigue. He made sure not to give her any cause for alarm.

She asked him to close the door when they entered her office. In a rare move, she instructed him to take a seat across from her. That was a sure sign he was about to be reprimanded, but Evan knew she was also worried about him fainting again.

"What are you doing here?" Before he could respond, she said, "I'm sorry, are you okay? How'd it go at the hospital?"

"I'm okay. My doctor wants to schedule a test for later this week. But she said I was fine. There's nothing I need to do in the meantime."

"Okay, that's great. Now, what are you doing here?"

He grinned at her.

She said, "I'm not smiling."

He wiped the smile off his face. "I came to get my car, thought I'd check with Jeremy before I left."

"Jeremy's doing fine. There's nothing going on here that requires you to come back to work, straight from the hospital."

He sighed. "Gwen, I understand what you're saying. And I know you probably won't understand what I'm about to tell you, but I need you to please hear me out. You know what's going on with my heart. You know how many times

I've been in the hospital. And you know just as well as I do that what happened earlier today is not a good sign.

"I've had this conversation with everyone who loves me, and I'm praying this will be the last time I have to do it — at least for today. I don't want to go home and wait to die. I don't mean to put this burden on you, but please don't make me do that."

She was stunned. His tone and the look in his eyes left her momentarily at a loss for words. Finally she said, "Evan, you're not dying. Don't talk like that."

"I'm not dying at this second, but I definitely have less days left than most men my age."

"Okay," she conceded. "But what does that have to do with you coming back to work today? It's four o'clock. What do you think you need to accomplish in an hour?"

"I just left the hospital. When you've been there as many times as I have, all for the same thing, you can't help but think about your mortality. Work is the one place I don't think about that. When I'm here, I feel young and productive and useful. I promise I won't do any heavy lifting, if you let me stay."

Gwen didn't find that amusing. She sighed. "I've got people in this department who'll call in for a hangnail. But the one person who probably needs to be at home won't leave."

"I don't need to be at home unless the doctor says so."

"Knowing you, he probably did tell you that, and you're not telling me."

"I wouldn't do that to you. If my cardiologist ever tells me to stay home, I'll stay home."

"Alright, Evan. But if you pass out again in my office, I'm sending you home until I speak to your cardiologist myself."

"If I get lightheaded, I'll make sure to put fifty feet between myself and your office," he assured her. "Thanks a lot, Gwen."

He left the office before she could reply to his dark humor or take back her permission for him to remain at the office.

After missing half the day at the hospital, Evan wanted to work past five, but Jeremy was eager to leave with the rest of the employees. Evan knew he'd be pushing Gwen too far, if he tried to work late by himself.

When he made it to the parking lot, he was surprised to see Sharelle parked in the same place she'd left him. She was so busy on her laptop, she didn't notice him approach her vehicle. She finally looked up and rolled the window down when she saw him standing there.

"Hey, Daddy."

"Um, did you forget something?"

"No, but I thought I'd stay to follow you home. You know, just in case..."

"Just in case I pass out behind the wheel?"

She shrugged. "Yeah."

He smiled. "Okay, honeybun."

She smiled too. "And when we get home, I can make you dinner."

"How about I make *you* dinner?"

"Okay."

"I might have to stop by a store, unless you want spaghetti. I think I have everything I need for that."

"Ooh, I love your spaghetti!"

"Great," he said. "It's a date."

When they got home, Evan got started on their meal, while Sharelle made herself comfortable at the kitchen table and continued plugging away at her homework. She talked a lot initially. Evan knew she was assessing him as much as she was keeping him company. He didn't mind.

He'd always been pleased that she chose to attend a local university, though he didn't let on at the time. Texas Lutheran was only thirty minutes away, but he and Delores had insisted their daughter live in the dorm. Not only was boarding part of her scholarship, but Evan felt it was a crucial part of college life. Sharelle visited almost every weekend and sometimes during the week too. Considering she was their only child, it was always nice to have her around.

Evan didn't begin to feel strange until his spaghetti was boiling, and he had ground beef browning in a skillet. Unlike the incident at work earlier that day, he was aware a dizzy spell was coming on. He checked to make sure Sharelle wasn't watching him before turning away from her slightly, as beads of sweat blossomed on his forehead. The frying pan swam out of focus, and the familiar gray and black dots took over his vision. He fought them off this time. He gripped the handle of the stove when his knees became weak.

His heart thundered. Evan didn't think it was his CHF causing his rapid heartbeats as much as it was his fear of death. He was not getting better. There was no denying it. After eight years, Dr. Davi had only slowed the progression of his ailment. She had not stopped it and most certainly had not reversed the damage already done.

And at that moment, Evan feared he'd pass out again, in front of his daughter this time, and when he woke up – *if* he woke up – she'd be in tears next to his bedside. His cardiologist would be talking about surgery again. Delores would be fraught with stress.

So Evan fought the dizziness, and when the floor settled beneath him, he surreptitiously wiped the sweat from his face. And when he dared to look over at Sharelle, he expected her to be staring at him with a knowing look in her eyes. Surely she'd seen everything, and she knew exactly what it all meant.

But his daughter hadn't looked away from her computer. She finally glanced in his direction when she realized he was watching her.

Her eyes narrowed, as she took in his features. "Everything okay?"

"Yeah. I was gonna ask what kind of sauce you want me to make. I came across a recipe for spicy Italian that I've been wanting to try."

"You know I love me some spicy food."

"Bet," he said. "I'll be done in about twenty minutes."

Delores called at six p.m. Evan was done cooking and setting the table by then. He checked the time but did not inquire about how long her attendance meeting after school had lasted.

"I'm on my way home. How are you feeling?"

"I'm good. Sharelle's here. I just made dinner. We're about to eat."

"You should be sitting down somewhere. Sharelle could've made dinner. Or I could've picked something up."

Evan did not want to continue arguing with people about his limitations. "Do you want us to wait on you, before we eat?"

"No, go ahead. I had a snack earlier. I'm not that hungry."

The lady of the house arrived with a flourish twenty minutes later. She entered from the garage and scarcely had time to put her laptop bag down before she hurried to the kitchen table, where Evan sat with Sharelle.

"Baby, I was so worried about you. Are you okay?" She hugged him from behind and kissed the side of his neck and cheek.

Delores was not as tall as her daughter, and her womanly physique wasn't as slim. She wore a skirt suit with a fashionable blouse that couldn't hide the swell of her large breasts, even though it was buttoned up and appropriate for her position at school. Likewise, her skirt exuded sexiness.

Though he couldn't see it at the moment, Evan remembered admiring her plump backside before she left for work that morning. She wore her hair down. Her makeup was scant, her skin complexion the color of a walnut shell.

As beautiful as she was, it was her drive that Evan found most attractive – until it became the only thing she cared about. Delores worked as a teacher for five years before getting her master's degree, so she could teach dual credit courses. She went back to school for a degree in education administration and quickly landed a spot as an assistant principal. She was currently working on her PhD.

"I would've left school early, if Sharelle wasn't here taking care of you," she said. "Thanks for coming," she told her daughter.

"I'm glad *somebody* appreciates it," Sharelle replied.

"You know I'm always happy to see you, honeybun," Evan told her. "I just don't like the *reason* I had to see you today."

"How was dinner?" Delores asked them.

"It was great," Sharelle replied. "Are you gonna have some?"

"I'm not supposed to be eating pasta right now, but I would like to spend time with my family."

"Great," Sharelle replied. "Wait, why aren't you eating pasta right now?"

"Would you believe she's dieting?" Evan answered.

"It's not a diet, it's a lifestyle," Delores quipped.

"Either way, I don't see why," Sharelle said. "You *fine*, Mama!"

"Ooh, thanks, girl!" Delores said. She did a quick spin and posed with a hand on her hip. "You know I gotta do something to keep them young gals away from my man."

She hugged Evan again. If Sharelle noticed the incredulous look on her father's face while his wife doted on him, she didn't comment on it.

Sharelle thought it might be a good idea to return home for the rest of the week, so someone would be there with Evan on the nights Delores had to work late. But he put his foot down and kept it down this time.

"I've had enough of the two of you emasculating me. I don't need a babysitter. If it gets to the point where I need home care, I'd rather have a nurse come over than pull you away from school."

"No one's trying to emasculate you," Delores said. "She's just trying to help."

Noticing the look on his daughter's face, Evan backtracked. "I'm sorry, baby girl. I've been telling people I'm alright all day. I don't mean to take it out on you. I'm just a little frustrated."

Sharelle was quick to accept his apology. "I understand, Daddy. I'm sorry for being so pushy. You know I'm only doing this because I love you."

Evan gave her a hug and a kiss on the cheek. "I know you do, honeybun. I'm sorry."

Sharelle left at eight, and Delores didn't speak much for the rest of the night. She saved her comments for when they got into bed. Evan was surprised that she chose to sleep with him tonight, but he didn't question it.

"That was a little rude, the way you spoke to Sharelle."

"I already apologized."

"What is it with you?" she pressed. "You've always had an independent streak, but it's gotten worse since you got sick."

"What is it with you, lying to Sharelle about your diet – or your lifestyle?"

"What? What are you talking about?"

"You know you're not worried about any *young gals* chasing me around. Everything you do for your appearance is for you."

"Evan, that's – I don't know why you're bringing that up. I was just kidding with her. What are you – did it bother you when I said that?"

He simmered but said, "No, I guess not."

"*Okay...*" She let the conversation go and shifted to an even more aggravating gear. "Do you think you'll need another surgery?"

Evan had already begun to accept that his last procedure, the angioplasty, hadn't fixed his heart. The last thing he wanted was to speak his worst fear out loud.

"We won't know until I have the ECHO. We'll see what Dr. Davi suggests after that."

"When you get sick like this, I just... I don't know what I'd do if I lost you."

Evan's heart bled for her until she added, "This isn't how my life is supposed to go."

He frowned in the darkness. "What do you mean?"

"Everything was going so well," she explained. "Our careers, Sharelle's in college. We have a beautiful home. Everything is perfect except..."

When she didn't finish her sentence, he said, "Except I'm sick."

She didn't respond. Evan assumed she was considering the callousness of her words, but he felt the need to drive the point home.

"I'm sorry my heart disease is interfering with your perfect life. I can assure you, it's interfering with mine a lot more."

"I'm just saying, I didn't sign up for this."

"Do you have any idea how much of a bitch you're being right now?"

She rolled away from him. "I don't know why I bothered trying to talk to you tonight. You already said you've been getting frustrated all day. First you take it out on Sharelle, and now you wanna take it out on me. Good night."

Evan's simmering blood began to boil. He hated how she cut off communication whenever *she* chose to. He didn't think he misinterpreted what she said, but she was right about him being aggravated before they got into bed. It was possible that he'd picked a fight with her, just so he could blow off some steam.

Either way, the stress he was putting himself through wasn't doing his heart any favors. He took ten deep breaths and released the bulk of his tension with each exhalation.

He told his wife, "I'm sorry," and rolled towards her instead of away.

"It's okay," she said as he spooned her from behind. "You know I love you."

"I love you too."

CHAPTER THREE
A BALLOON IN MY WHAAAT?

On Wednesday, Evan returned to the hospital for his echocardiogram. Delores didn't offer to go with him, and Evan was okay with that. He had the procedure performed several times in the past eight years. It was noninvasive and didn't require any sedation. He told her she could sit this one out. He arrived alone and quickly made it through registration. Thirty minutes later, he lie on an exam table with a technician applying electrodes to his bare skin.

"Try to lie still and breath naturally," she instructed. "Dr. Davi wants a view from the front and the side. I'll let you know when it's time to roll over."

"Do you know how long it will take to get the results?" Evan asked.

"Dr. Davi is in the office," the tech informed him. "She wants you to stay here when I get done, to give her time to look at the images. You'll have a chance to speak with her before you leave."

After the procedure, Evan was sent to a waiting room. He remained there for 45 minutes, before he was called to the front desk again. A PCT led him to a different exam room and left him alone for a few minutes until Dr. Davi made her appearance.

"Good morning, Evan. How are you?"

"To be honest, I'm on pins and needles," he said. "I had another dizzy spell when I went home last night. I didn't pass out, but I started sweating. I felt like I was close to falling."

The cardiologist nodded as she uploaded images on a portable computer. A few moments later, colored pictures of his heart that looked like ultrasound images filled a large screen mounted on the wall. For Evan, the pictures were indecipherable. But they held a wealth of information for his cardiologist.

"We're still having trouble with the left side of your heart," Dr. Davi announced. "Your medication has slowed the progress of your heart disease, but if you look here..."

She pointed with a mouse. Evan followed the clicker, but the images still didn't make sense to him.

"You can see the disease spreading further right," his cardiologist continued. "I think the meds you're taking are helping. Things would've progressed a lot faster if they weren't. But I'm worried they have not stopped the spread of the disease. Ideally, we'd like to see the damage reversed."

Evan felt a sense of déjà vu. He had the same thoughts last night.

"What's worse," the doctor said, "we're having trouble with your tricuspid valve. For your last procedure, I performed angioplasty on your left coronary artery. The stent has held up, but this valve is a bigger problem. It controls the blood flow from your left atrium to your left ventricle. The valve has become stiff, and it's not opening properly. This is why you're starting to see symptoms, such as sweating, palpitations and shortness of breath. As this condition worsens, you'll experience dizzy spells. In severe cases, you'll pass out."

At the beginning of his diagnosis, Evan wouldn't have understood the difference between a ventricle and an ankle bone. Now he could picture the things going on in his heart, especially with the visuals Dr. Davi provided.

His blood ran cold. "You, you said if I pass out, that out means it's severe?"

The cardiologist's demeanor became as somber as her news. "Yes, Evan. I'm sorry."

Evan couldn't say he was surprised by any of this, but the news still floored him. He wondered what this meant, as far as the years he had left to live. Or was he down to months. He dared not ask.

"What's next?" he asked instead. "Where do we go from here?"

"I recommend a procedure called valvuloplasty." The doctor handed him a pamphlet. She was quiet for a few moments, while Evan read it and looked at the graphics.

He couldn't help but frown at what he was seeing. "What is that – a balloon?"

"Yes," the cardiologist confirmed. "I would insert a catheter through the valve. A portion of the catheter will have a small balloon that I will inflate to open the valve. I may have to inflate it a few times, until the valve opens. When it's open, I'll remove the catheter." Noticing his expression, she told him, "If we don't take action on this, it will lead to a heart attack."

Evan felt like he might have a heart attack from the news she was giving him. Of all the horrible things this woman had told him about his most crucial organ, she never used the phrase *heart attack* before.

"Will, will this procedure fix everything?"

He knew the answer before asking. His cardiologist became even more subdued.

"Evan, this procedure will only take care of what's currently going on with your tricuspid valve. Curing your heart disease is the only way to fix everything. That's what we're hoping the medication, therapy and your immune system will do over time."

"I could have a heart attack if I don't do this?"

"It's not a matter of *could*, Evan. It's a matter of *when*."

He swallowed audibly. "Then it doesn't sound like I have a choice."

Her disposition brightened. "Don't sound so gloomy. The valvuloplasty will take care of the symptoms you currently have, which is a big deal. I'm confident your heart will heal over time. But healing is not only accomplished with procedures and medicine. It takes a positive outlook as well."

"Okay," Evan said, attempting to match her optimism. "Then let's do it. When do you think I should have it done?"

"I would like to do it today. You're at risk for a heart attack every day we wait."

His eyes widened. "Okay."

"I have to let you know there are risks involved with this procedure. They are outlined in the pamphlet, but the most serious ones are blood clots, leakage at the valve, rupture of the valve – which would require open heart surgery – stroke, kidney failure or death. You have to sign a consent form before I begin."

Evan's pupils remained dilated. "Okay…"

"I know that all sounds scary, but those are only *possible* risks. The for sure outcome if we don't do the procedure is a heart attack."

Evan didn't think she needed to drive that point home any further. "Okay. I'll sign the consent."

"Great. You can do that up front. When you're done, we'll prep you for the procedure. We'll use local anesthetics, and you'll remain awake the whole time. Afterwards, if everything goes well, we'll send you to cardiac telemetry for a day or so to recover."

That was the only good news she had given him that morning. If he returned to C3, that meant he wasn't dying, plus he'd have an opportunity to see his bestie. It was a stay on the first two floors he had to worry about.

"Alright, doctor. I trust you. I'm ready."

Before they prepped him for the procedure, Evan called his wife. She surprised him by answering after a couple of rings.

"Hey, how'd it go? What'd they say?"

"My heart disease is getting worse," he reported. "Dr. Davi says one of my valves isn't opening, which is why I passed out. She wants to do another procedure called valvuloplasty. It's like the angioplasty, but instead of a stent, she'll insert a balloon that will force the valve open."

After a pause, Delores asked, "Is that a permanent fix, or will another valve or artery collapse next month?"

Evan had wondered the same thing, so he couldn't fault her for asking. But he thought the comment was a little calloused.

"If my CHF doesn't get better, my whole heart will stop working. So, no, this might not be a permanent fix. But the doctor says I could have a heart attack at any moment, if I don't have this done."

His wife paused again before saying, "Well, I guess we have to do it, then."

Again, her response mirrored his own, but Evan expected more compassion.

"When does she want to do it?" Delores asked.

"Today, in about an hour."

"Oh, that soon?"

"You know how it's been going with me; I come in for a checkup and end up needing something that will keep me here for days."

"Yeah, that does seem to be the case."

Evan bristled at her comment. He didn't need a pity party, but he also didn't need her to be so quick to agree with him. Would it kill her to talk him off a ledge every now and then?

When she asked, "Do you need me to come now, before they start?"

He was quick to tell her, "No. It's not surgery. They'll use local anesthetics and go in through the groin, like last time. They're sending me to C3 afterwards. It's not a big deal."

"Okay," she said. "If you don't want me to come, I'll come see you after work."

Evan frowned. Her statement sounded scripted, like something she might use against him later.

He told her, "That's fine."

"Okay. I love you."

"I love you too."

The procedure went well. Evan appreciated being awake the whole time, but his consciousness left plenty of time to consider the wonder of a doctor inserting a catheter in his groin, injecting dye that made the blood vessel easy to follow on monitors that provided live x-ray images, and guiding the catheter all the way to his heart. The doctor navigated the balloon tip to the faulty valve and told Evan, "You may feel some discomfort," as she inflated it.

She told him, "Let me know if you have shortness of breath, difficulty breathing or chest pain."

Evan expected the worst, but he only experienced dizziness and brief chest discomfort. He told the cardiologist, "It's okay. I'm good."

He wasn't sure how many times she had to inflate the balloon. Finally she told him, "Okay, I got the valve open, and it appears to be functioning properly. I'm going to remove the catheter now."

She withdrew it slowly. The feeling of a foreign object sliding the length of his blood vessel was not a sensation he could get used to. He blew out a sigh of relief when she told him, "Okay, Evan, I'm out. You're not bleeding very badly at the insertion sight, so we don't need sutures to close the opening. I'm going to have Carl apply pressure, and then he'll wrap it with a bandage. I need you to remain lying flat for a couple of hours. If this becomes uncomfortable, I can give you something to help you relax."

When the surgical assistant stepped close enough for her to back away and allow him to apply pressure, Dr. Davi approached the head of the bed and looked down at her patient. Because of her surgical mask, Evan couldn't see her mouth, but her eyes were smiling.

"You did great, Evan. How do you feel?"

"It wasn't as bad as I expected," he said gruffly.

"Good. Once Carl gets your leg wrapped up, they'll take you up to C3. The insertion site on your groin will take the longest to heal. I don't want you to bend your leg for several hours. I know you emptied your bladder before the procedure, but if you have to pee soon, we'll have to get you a catheter."

Evan frowned at that. "I don't have to go, and if the need arises, I'll hold it until you say I can stand up. I'm done with catheters, doc, hopefully for the rest of my life."

She chuckled and patted his shoulder. "Don't worry. We'll get you better, Evan. You'll be back to your old self in no time. I'll come up and see you in a few hours."

"Okay, doctor. Thank you. I appreciate everything you do."

Evan got settled in his room on C3 an hour after his procedure. Once there, he only had to wait thirty minutes before a ray of sunshine brightened his day. His longtime nurse Jada Kirkland came to check on him while a PCT was taking his vitals.

"There's my favorite patient! How are you Evan?"

Jada's smile was broad and genuine. She wore the royal blue scrub suit required for all nurses at the hospital. Her skin tone was a shade lighter than Evan's. She rocked her shoulder-length, frizzy hair natural. Though her scrubs didn't accentuate her figure, other nurses (and sometimes patients) often complimented her slim physique. The little makeup she wore was blended well.

The hospital recognized the importance of continuity of care, so Evan was assigned to this floor whenever bed availability made it possible. Likewise, whenever he arrived on the unit, Jada was tasked with overseeing his medical regimen. Over the past eight years, he had been her patient over a dozen times.

"I'm not great," he told her. "But I made it through another procedure. I'm thankful for that."

"Yes, you did!" his nurse exclaimed. "I talked to Dr. Davi a few minutes ago. She said it went very well."

"I hope this is the last of it. I'm a little sick of these hospital stays."

"Aww, is it really that bad? It's the only time I get to see you," she joked.

Evan smiled at that. "Yeah, you're right. With that in mind, I guess it's not that bad."

The tech finished gathering the information she needed.

"Everything looks good," she said to the nurse and the patient as she wheeled her portable computer out of the room. "You missed lunch," she told Evan, "but Dr. Davi doesn't want you to eat anyway, not for a few hours. Think you can hold out that long?"

"I didn't eat breakfast either," Evan told her. "I was too nervous. But I'm not hungry now. I'll be alright."

When the PCT stepped out of the room, Jada slipped on a pair of gloves and walked closer to the bed. "I'm going to take a look at your leg."

He nodded, and she lifted the sheet covering his lower body. Evan was nude beneath his hospital gown. To assess the bandage around his upper thigh, she had to lift his gown past his hips, partially exposing his genitals. She did so with clinical detachment.

"They wrapped you up tight," she noticed. "Are you in any pain?"

"It hurts a little," he acknowledged. "Inserting the catheter was more uncomfortable than inflating that balloon in my heart."

Her delicate fingers moved about his bandage and the blood vessel that disappeared beneath it.

"The blood flow looks good," she said. "I won't know if there's any bruising until we unwrap it. Dr. Davi doesn't want you up walking for another two hours. If you need to go to the bathroom–"

"Nope. I already told her I don't want another catheter – especially not *there*."

Jada grinned at him and possibly blushed. She lowered his gown and blanket. She removed her gloves and washed her hands at a sink in the room. She returned to him and placed her hands on the bedrail. Evan looked down at her delicate fingers before meeting her eyes.

"I know you don't want to be here," she told him. "I get it. You are one of my favorite patients, but I'd be happy if you never came back. That way I'd know you got better."

"Hey, you said I was your favorite patient, not *one of* your favorites."

"Well, you know a nurse isn't supposed to play favorites. A teacher can't have a favorite student either."

"None of the other patients are here to get jealous. It's okay if you say I'm your favorite."

"I like it when you smile," she said. "That means you feel better. Did..." Her smile ebbed a little as she looked around the room. She thought his visitors may have stepped out for a second, but she didn't see anyone's personal belongings on any of the empty chairs.

"Did you come to the hospital alone today?"

He nodded. "Yeah. Dr. Davi gave me a pamphlet, and the procedure didn't seem that complicated. I didn't want anyone to miss school or work for this."

Jada didn't respond to that. She knew the valvuloplasty was extremely complicated. If something had gone wrong, she would've hated for Evan to be in distress without his support system. Thankfully, everything went through without a hitch.

"I'll be back in a little while to remove your bandage. If you're still bleeding, Dr. Davi may have to suture the insertion sight, but I think we'll be alright."

"Okay," Evan told her. "Thank you."

she was pleased to see the blood had clotted properly, and there was no bleeding. Evan was glad to have the bandage removed, because despite not having many fluids that morning, he really had to go. Jada assisted him as he got out of bed. She cautioned him not to put a lot of weight on his leg. Evan held on to the rails around the toilet, and his nurse stepped out to give him privacy. She helped him back into bed before leaving to attend to other patients.

When her shift ended at 7pm, she gave report to the nurse relieving her. Before she left for the day, she stopped by Evan's room. She was surprised to find he was still alone.

"I'm about to take off," she said as she approached his bed. "Your nighttime nurse is Tamara. She'll be in to check on you in a little while. How was dinner? Did you get enough to eat?"

"It was great," he replied. "Your cafeteria has stepped up their game. I don't remember the food being that good the last time I was here. Or maybe I was just hungry."

"You said you didn't eat breakfast today," she recalled. "So maybe it was a combination of the two." She paused briefly to consider her next question. "How's Sharelle?" she asked, looking for a way to ease into what she was really curious about.

"She's great," Evan said, his face brightening. "She's finishing up her junior year at Texas Lutheran. Their basketball team isn't very good, but her grades are awesome. Did I tell you she's a business major?"

Seeing the way he lit up while discussing his daughter made Jada's heart sigh. "No, I think you said she was undecided the last time you were here."

"Yeah, I think she's found her niche. I can't wait to watch her take the world by storm."

"That's great! I'm happy for her. I was hoping to see her today. Do you think she'll stop by tomorrow?"

Evan grinned sheepishly. "She would've stopped by already, if she knew I was here."

Jada raised an eyebrow.

"I didn't tell her I was coming today," Evan explained. "I knew she would've left school to be here with me, and I didn't want that. She spends too much time trying to take care of me. I would rather she focus on being young and in college."

Jada nodded. "That's understandable."

"Trust me, when she calls tonight and finds out where I am, she won't be happy. She might still have an attitude by the time you see her tomorrow."

Jada chuckled at that. "I'll bet she will. Is Delores gonna have an attitude too? I can't believe you didn't tell her either..."

"No, she knows I'm here. I talked to her before the procedure."

He didn't elaborate on that, so Jada didn't feel she was in a position to question him further. But she did check the time, almost subconsciously. It was after seven pm. Unless Delores had another career change since the last time Evan was at the hospital, she was still an assistant principal at a local high school. At the latest, school would've let out at four. Jada couldn't imagine a scenario that would've kept Mrs. Shales away from her husband during or after his procedure.

But being his nurse didn't automatically make her his confidant. All of her patients had things going on in their lives that she wasn't privy to. In this case, it was probably better that way.

"Alright, well, I'll be back tomorrow morning. Hopefully Dr. Davi will sign off on you by noon, and you won't have to spend another night here."

"I don't know," Evan kidded. "You guys are treating me so good, I might want to stay another day."

Jada's smile returned. "That's our job. I'll take that to mean we're doing it well. Good night, Evan." Before she backed out of the room, she told him, "I know it's weird to say this, but it always makes me happy to see you, even though it usually means something went wrong with your heart."

He grinned. "I feel that way too. I've known you longer than a lot of people in my life. When I think of some of the talks we've had over the years, how you've been there for my laughter and my tears, I feel like we're closer than some of my best friends."

Her eyes glistened. "I feel that way too, Evan."

"I'm glad you're always my nurse," he said. "I can't imagine developing this kind of relationship with someone else."

Her smile widened. "Me neither. Get some rest. I'll see you in the morning."

"Okay. Good night, Jada. Sleep well."

CHAPTER FOUR
DIVA

Delores walked into Evan's hospital room a little after nine pm. She wore sneakers, a Pink jogging suit and a coat to ward off the January freeze. She toted her laptop bag and what Evan assumed was an overnight bag.

"Sorry it took me so long. I had to stop by the house to get my things, so I can spend the night with you." She deposited her bags on a chair and walked to his bed. She pecked him on the lips. "How you feeling?"

When she backed away, Evan eyed her warily. He wondered, not for the first time, if she might be having an affair. He never questioned her before, and he chose not to do it now. Instead, he told her, "I appreciate you coming, but you don't have to spend the night. I know you have to get to work pretty early."

"I wish you would've told me that before I went home and got all my things together."

"Sorry. I haven't talked to you too much today."

"I'm sorry, baby. This was a day from hell. I got so much going on at school. Did you get something to eat? I think the cafeteria is still open. I can go down and get you something right quick."

"I already ate. Did you have dinner yet?"

"I stopped by Chick-Fil-A and got a salad. Don't know why I tried to eat that while I was driving. Got salad dressing on my tan slacks. But the salad was good, though. Where's your call button? Is your cardiologist still here? Have they given you an update yet?"

"Who do you need me to call?" Evan asked.

"Your nurse. I wanna know what's going on, and I'ma need a cot in here, some blankets too."

"I got an update from Dr. Davi earlier today. I told you the procedure went well. She's going to come see me tomorrow morning."

"You haven't had an update since this afternoon? They've got to have more information than that. What are you spending the night for, if everything is good?"

Rather than wait for him to press his call button, she reached over him and pressed it herself.

"I don't think you're supposed to use that unless there's a problem," Evan said.

"It's a nurse call button," Delores countered. "I wanna talk to your nurse. That's what it's for."

"The nurse's station is right out—"

"Can I help you?" a voice asked over the call button.

"Yes," Delores said. "I would like to speak to my husband's nurse."

"Is there something wrong?" the woman on the other end of the speaker asked.

"No, but I would like to get updated information on his condition. And I need a cot in here, so I can spend the night, some pillows and blankets too."

"Ma'am, this is not what the call button is for."

Evan rolled his eyes.

"You need to come to the nurses' station to request a cot and blankets," the voice continued. "Evan's nurse is here too, if you need to speak to her."

"I know what the call button is for," Delores snapped. She leaned over him to get closer to the speaker. "This isn't my first time in a hospital. If you don't want to help me, put someone on the line who can."

After a pause and an audible sigh, the woman said, "Okay, ma'am. One moment."

Evan cringed at his wife's diva-like behavior. The people at the hospital had been so good to him.

"I always have problems with the night shift," Delores complained as she took a seat across from him. "I know it's not easy to work overnight, but they can get another job, if it's too stressful for them."

Evan didn't respond to that.

His nightshift nurse stepped into the room a moment later. Tamara wore the same smile she had when she greeted him earlier in the shift. Evan wondered if she had no idea what she was stepping into or if she was a good actress.

"Hi," she said to Delores. "You wanted to speak to me?"

"Yes. I would like updated information on my husband's condition. The lady up front is acting like that's too much of an inconvenience for her."

"I'm sorry for that," the nurse said. She remained calm and cool. "Evan is being held overnight for observation. He had a valvuloplasty this morning. His blood vessel looks good at the insertion site, and his cardiologist said the procedure went well. We're keeping him overnight to make sure his tricuspid valve continues to function properly, and we don't observe any abnormal EKG rhythms.

We haven't seen any so far. I'm sure Dr. Davi will discharge him by lunchtime tomorrow."

"Thank you," Delores said. "I also asked about getting a cot and some pillows and a blanket, so I can spend the night with him."

"Okay. I'll have a tech bring that for you."

"Thank you," Delores said again. "What's your name?" She checked her ID badge and answered the question herself. "Tamara?"

"Yes."

"I like you, Tamara."

"Thank you, ma'am. Let me know if you need anything else."

The nurse retreated, leaving the husband and wife alone.

"How was your day?" he asked her. "What made it a day from hell?"

"It was okay, nothing I can't handle."

She retrieved her laptop and opened it on her lap. Within seconds, she was either scrutinizing what she saw on the screen or click-clacking away on the keyboard. She was so busy, she barely acknowledged the PCT when she brought the cot and blanket she requested.

She told her, "Thank you, dear," without looking up.

Evan waited thirty more minutes before asking her, "Why'd you bother coming?"

She looked up at him.

"Hmm? Why would you ask that?"

"It's a fair question. I wanna know what your goal is. What do you expect to accomplish?"

"I'm not trying to accomplish anything. Is it wrong for me to spend the night at the hospital with my husband?"

"In theory, no," he said. "But if you intended to comfort your husband, make him feel loved, make him feel like he's not cooped up in a hospital with no one to talk to, you're not doing a good job."

She sighed. "Evan, you know I'm working on my PhD. You know how hard it is for me to get this work done and work a full-time job. I'm juggling a lot of things right now. Sometimes I have to multitask."

"I appreciate you coming here and allowing me to watch you work," he said. "But it's not necessary. I've been doing fine by myself all day."

Delores pursed her lips, and then her features softened. She closed her laptop and returned it to the bag. She bent to untie her shoes before stepping gingerly to his bed. She sat next to him and placed a hand on his chest.

She stared into his eyes sheepishly and said, "I'm sorry."

He frowned at her.

She smiled and caressed his chest tenderly. "My big bear needs some attention," she said in a sing-song voice. "I'm not being a good wifey. *I'm sowwy.*"

Evan didn't appreciate her patronizing him, but his heart responded to her nearness, no matter how hard his brain tried to reject it. He grinned, despite himself.

He told her, "You're being a bitch."

"*Oh no*," she said, pretending to be offended. "I'm being a bitch to you or these hot-tailed nurses you got running around here?"

"Hot-tailed?"

"I know they all want some *Mr. Shales*. But they ain't gon' get him. That's why I had to come up here and let these ho's know you're spoken for."

Evan couldn't take her seriously. If she was so worried about losing him to another woman, why not do something simple, like show him she loved him?

"Are you gonna scoot over, so I can lay with you?" she asked. "Or are you sending me home?"

When he didn't respond, she slowly unzipped her jacket, revealing a thin camisole beneath. Evan momentarily got lost in the swell of her breasts. He scooted over to make room for her.

Delores removed her jacket. She lifted his blanket and lie next to him. The hospital bed wasn't very large, but it was big enough to accommodate both of them. She lie on her side, facing him. Evan remained on his back. She draped an arm over his chest, careful not to knock any of his electrodes off the sticky pads. She kissed him on the neck.

She said, "Do you want me to tell you about my day from hell?"

Though his emotions were conflicted, his desire for companionship was not.

"Yeah. Tell me."

They talked for thirty minutes before falling asleep.

When Jada arrived on the unit the next morning, she was pleased to encounter Evan's wife. Mrs. Shales was smartly dressed, with a travel bag draped over her shoulder and a laptop bag in hand. She was headed for the elevators, presumably on her way to work. Jada thought she was a beautiful woman.

"Good morning," she told her.

It had been a year since they last met, but Delores stopped for a moment when recognition dawned.

"Good morning. You're Evan's nurse, aren't you?"

"Yes, I'm Jada, his dayshift nurse. How was he last night?"

"He slept like a baby," Delores said. "I think he's doing a lot better. I hope they let him go home soon."

"We're expecting him to be discharged today. Dr. Davi wanted to make sure he didn't have any cardiac events overnight. She might want to do another ECHO this morning, to check his valve again."

Delores frowned. "*Another* ECHO? How much is that gonna cost?"

Jada frowned as well. "I, um, I don't know anything about the financial side. You'll have to check with the billing office."

Delores sighed with a shake of her head. "Y'all a little *extra* sometimes. Be doing the most."

Jada didn't know how to respond to that. Thankfully she didn't have to. Delores walked past her, and Jada continued to the nurses' station.

Dr. Davi checked with her patient and Evan's nurse at 11 a.m. She did not see a need for another ECHO. Thirty minutes later, Jada came to Evan's room with news she knew would make him happy.

"Good morning. You ready to go home?"

His face didn't light up like she expected. He was sitting on the side of the bed. His breakfast tray sat on a stand to his right. Jada noticed it had barely been touched.

"Yeah, I guess so," he replied.

"*You guess so*?" she said with a smile. "Yesterday you couldn't wait to get out of here."

"I do want to get out of here." He noticed the papers in her hand. "Are those my discharge orders?"

Jada wanted to talk more about why he seemed down, but she said, "Yes. Dr. Davi is changing one of your meds, and she wants you to start physical therapy to strengthen your heart..."

Three minutes later, she was done reviewing the orders. Evan didn't seem like he'd been paying attention while she talked. Sure enough, the first thing he asked her when she finished was, "Do you remember the first time I was admitted to this unit?"

Jada cocked her head slightly. "Well, I don't remember the exact date, but I know it was about eight years ago."

He nodded. "That's almost a decade. The first time I came, I had a little chest pain. I thought it was a severe case of indigestion. But it turned out to be CHF."

Jada nodded.

"Eight years later," he continued, "I'm still dealing with the same issue. You've been my nurse, pretty much the whole time."

She continued to nod. "Yes, I have."

"Each time I see you, a part of me hopes it will be the last time," he said.

"Really?" she joked. "You don't like seeing me?"

His tone remained serious. "Actually, seeing you is the only part of this experience I don't hate."

"Aww. That's sweet. That means I'm doing a good job."

Evan's eyebrows bunched slightly. He wasn't sure why, but he felt dejected each time she referred to their time together as her *job*. She was a nurse, and he was her patient. Their interactions were basically transactional. There was nothing wrong with her acknowledging that.

"What's really bothering you?" she asked.

He sighed, looking into her eyes. "I'm worried that I'm not getting better, and I don't want to be a burden."

This was the second time he'd told her that. Jada knew it wasn't a flippant comment. Her tone matched his when she asked, "Why do you keep saying that? Who do you feel like you're a burden to?"

"My family. I already told you I don't like it when my daughter leaves school to be with me when I'm sick."

She continued to watch his eyes. "Did she come last night?"

He shook his head. "No. She still doesn't know I'm here. She usually calls me every day, or every other day, just to say hi, let me know how she's doing. Yesterday I was in an uncomfortable position – wanting to hear from her and *not* wanting to at the same time. I was glad she didn't call, so I wouldn't have to tell her I was in the hospital. I don't like feeling that way."

Jada took a deep breath. "I understand."

"And my wife," he continued, "I know I'm a burden to her. Remember the things I told you last year? I feel like it's getting worse."

Jada felt like continuing the conversation would be treading into hazardous waters. She was hesitant to ask.

"Why do you feel like your illness is a burden to her?"

"Because she's got a lot going on. She's always busy. She worries about the medical bills piling up. I know it's a lot to deal with, physically and mentally – not to mention the financial side."

Jada considered what Delores had said when she passed her in the hallway that morning. She knew there was some truth to what Evan was saying, and she knew she shouldn't comment on problems he may be having with his spouse. In the past, when he voiced similar concerns, she was careful to listen and not offer any advice. She smiled, hoping to lighten the mood.

"You shouldn't worry about those things, Evan. Your wife loves you. And marriage is for better or worse. It'll be alright."

He surprised her by chuckling at that. He looked down at her hand. Noticing her bare ring finger, he said, "How come you're not wearing your ring? Is everything okay with your marriage?"

Jada couldn't maintain her smile. After a pause, she said, "I haven't been wearing it for a while, Evan. I'm divorced."

"Oh, I, uh. I'm sorry I haven't noticed."

"It's okay."

"I guess marriage isn't always for better or worse then, is it?"

Evan regretted his words immediately, especially as he watched a flood of emotions mar his nurse's delicate features. The pain in her eyes was undeniable.

"I'm–"

Before he could apologize, a patient transporter entered the room, pushing a wheelchair ahead of him.

"Mr. Shales, I'm here to take you downstairs for discharge."

"Great," Jada said. Her smile returned in an instant. "He's ready to go. Get better soon," she said to Evan as she backed out of the room. "I predict this will be the last time I see you; your heart is gonna get super strong. Enjoy the rest of your day."

She was as cheery as ever, but Evan didn't think she'd ever addressed him so coldly. He wanted to tell her he was against this being their last encounter, but he knew that would be inappropriate, especially with the transporter in the room.

Instead he said, "Thank you, Jada. I hope you have a nice day too."

CHAPTER FIVE

THIS VALVE OF MINE

Evan made it six months before tragedy struck.

He'd gotten back into the swing of things and felt he was getting his life back on track. His physical therapy had gone well. He couldn't run a five-minute mile, but his heart felt healthy. Dr. Davi told him everything looked good during their last follow up appointment.

Delores hadn't been cold towards him, but Evan guessed that was because he hadn't put her in a position she was uncomfortable with. She hadn't had to care for him or visit him at the hospital. They had outstanding medical bills, but this wasn't a cause for stress. The hospital approved a payment plan that didn't upend their budget. The expense was like an extra car payment, which was something they'd managed comfortably when they bought Sharelle her first car.

Evan's daughter and his work at T9 Solutions continued to be the highlights of his life. He couldn't have been more proud of Sharelle, and he and Jeremy continued to produce stellar ads for companies as big as Apple and Walmart. They'd begun to brainstorm the groundwork required if they decided to leave T9 and start their own business. One of the main reasons for Evan's hesitance was the great insurance package their employer provided. He was wary about looking for a new provider with his pre-existing medical condition.

He was mowing the lawn on a particularly hot July afternoon when his sweat, which was moderate at the time, seemed to freeze over. He reached to wipe his brow and felt pain in his left arm and shoulder. Unexpectedly, his knees buckled. Suddenly unsteady on his feet, he gripped the handle of the lawn mower but still couldn't stop himself from dropping to one knee. A sudden sensation of nausea was so powerful, he dry heaved.

Evan knew what was happening to him immediately, and while the symptoms were exactly what Dr. Davi warned him to look out for, they were nothing like the way it was portrayed on TV. Rather than severe chest pain, there was pressure and tightening behind his sternum. He didn't feel the need to clutch his chest and cry out to a dead relative, like Redd Foxx popularized.

But his fear was crippling, even more than the pain. The knowledge that he was most likely having a heart attack brought with it the realization that his treatment had failed. He wasn't getting better. And given the damage his heart disease had already wreaked on his most precious organ, it was unlikely he would survive this. He envisioned his death on the front lawn, beneath the blistering July sun. He would never see his family in Washington again. He wouldn't be around for Sharelle's graduation.

This understanding made tears glint in his eyes as the pain in his chest became more severe. A grimace distorted his features as his hand slipped from the lawnmower. Without pressure on the throttle control, the machine stopped immediately, and the whole neighborhood became quiet. Evan planted both hands in the freshly cut grass and tried to call out to Delores. The last time he'd seen her, she was inside working on her thesis. His heart attack did not render him completely mute, but he could not produce the volume required for her to hear him through the front door. But still, he tried.

"Delores. Help me. Delores."

Even to him, his hoarse cries for help sounded more like a death rattle. Around him, the world spun at a dizzying speed, revolving a full 180 degrees. Evan didn't realize it was actually him that was moving until the side of his face impacted the soft lawn. Now he was hot. So very hot. Beads of sweat trickled down his face and into his eyes, temporarily blinding him. He blinked quickly to clear his vision, but when he opened his eyes again, he still couldn't see. He wondered if the sweat was actually blood.

In a strange bit of irony, he saw a dead relative, as his life flashed before his eyes. The last time he'd seen his grandmother Eunice, he was ten years old. Her memory should've been as foggy as the rest of his vision, but she was the only thing he could see clearly. She spoke to him. Evan couldn't hear what she was saying, but after a while, he found he could read her lips. What she was saying was so chilling, his fractured heartbeats stopped altogether. Rather than telling him everything would be alright, Eunice had her arm outstretched, reaching for him.

She was calling him home.

A neighbor found him in the lawn. It was uncertain how long Evan had been there, hoarsely crying out for help. Mrs. Freeman, a retiree, ran first to her downed neighbor and then to the front of the house. She jabbed the doorbell frantically while fishing her cellphone from her purse. Evan's first realization that he was not dead was a vision of Delores rushing from the house. Mrs. Freeman was frantic, and Evan's wife quickly followed suit. Evan thought it took an enormous amount of time before an ambulance arrived, while his wife spoke with the 9-1-1 operator and attempted to assess his condition. But eventually, he did hear sirens in the distance.

"*He's breathing,*" he heard Delores say into the phone. "*I think he's breathing. Please God, don't let him die.*"

Evan didn't remember losing consciousness, but at some point, he must have. When he awakened, he found himself on the first floor of Jackson Memorial's cardiac tower. Cardiac ICU was a unit he dreaded. He'd only been there once in eight years. During that stay, he heard several Code Blue's announced over the hospital intercom and saw nurses rushing past his door, hoping to save a patient who had stopped breathing. After one of these events, he saw patient transporters roll a covered body off the unit.

When he awakened, he saw Delores sitting near his bedside. Sharelle stood next to him, as if her love alone could will him to wake up. The tears in her eyes broke what was left of Evan's heart. He knew guilt shouldn't be his overriding emotion after what he'd experienced, but he loved his daughter much more than he loved himself. She didn't deserve a father who was constantly knocking on death's door.

Noticing his eyes flutter open, Sharelle said, "Daddy? You're awake?"

He nodded weakly. His voice was hoarse when he replied. "Yeah, baby. I'm okay."

His declaration did not fill her with confidence. Fresh tears spilled down her cheeks.

"Mom!" she said, without looking away from him. "He's awake!"

Delores stood and came to her daughter's side.

Evan asked them, "Did I have a heart attack?"

Delores nodded solemnly.

Sharelle said, "Yes, Daddy. How do you feel?"

She reached for his hand. Evan welcomed her touch. Within seconds, their fingers were interlocked.

"I feel okay," he told her. "I don't know what happened. One minute I was mowing the lawn. The next second, I was laying in it."

"You shouldn't have been mowing, if you didn't feel good," Sharelle said.

"I, I didn't feel anything before I started," he explained. He had to take a couple of breaths to recoup from the little he had spoken. He was surprised by how exhausted he was.

"Don't try to talk, Daddy. You need to rest. I'm gonna go get your nurse. She told us to let her know when you woke up."

"I'll go," Delores offered. "You stay with your father."

Evan watched his wife's eyes but was unable to get a read on her reaction to his heart attack or him being in the hospital again. His gaze returned to his daughter's wet orbs, which were quite the opposite.

"Okay," Sharelle said without looking back. "I love you, Daddy. I'm so glad you're okay."

After a brief assessment by his nurse, Evan's cardiologist arrived on the unit and performed an evaluation of her own. Evan wasn't surprised Dr. Davi wanted another ECHO. After the procedure, he was sent back to his room, where his wife and daughter waited anxiously. By then, they had delivered dinner to all of the patients. Evan didn't have an appetite, but Sharelle implored him to try to eat. He ate half his portion of spaghetti casserole and an equal amount of his diner roll before telling her he was stuffed. An hour later, Dr. Davi returned with a new prognosis.

"Would you like to speak to me alone?" the cardiologist asked, noticing Evan had visitors.

He looked from Sharelle to his wife. He would actually prefer Sharelle not be in the room when the doctor told him what was wrong with him, but that day, she had been far more emotionally invested in his wellbeing than Delores. Evan felt it would be wrong to ask his daughter to leave.

"No, they're family," he said. "You can speak in front of them."

Dr. Davi nodded. "Evan, your tricuspid valve has become stenotic, meaning it's stiff and not opening as it should to allow blood to pass through. Your heart is working hard to compensate, but with your heart disease, frankly its not strong enough to do extra work. The last time I saw trouble with this valve, I performed the valvuloplasty. I forced the valve open, and it began to work on its own. Your valve is now worse than it was when I performed that procedure. We could try it again, but that is not my recommendation."

Stunned, Evan took a deep breath and blew it out slowly. Now that he knew what was going on in his chest, he could almost feel his stiff valve impeding the blood flow.

"To make matters worse," the doctor continued, "the cardiac episode you had today further damaged your heart. At this point, I recommend a heart valve replacement surgery. We would remove your tricuspid valve and replace it with a valve made of carbon coated plastic."

Evan's eyes widened. Sharelle's did to. He heard her gasp loudly enough for the doctor to hear it.

"Ideally, we would like to replace the valve with one from a donor," Dr. Davi went on. "But I do not believe you would be approved for that. Given your advanced heart disease, it is likely that other parts of your heart will require attention within the next few years. A valve from a donor is recommended for patients who have a problem with *one valve only* and have an otherwise healthy heart. From the images I saw today, your heart disease has begun to spread from the left to the right side."

If he wasn't so weak, that news would've caused Evan to sit up with a jolt.

"Unfortunately, I would not expect you to live more than three to six months without the valve replacement," the cardiologist said. "With the surgery, we can buy you a few years, to see if the medicine and therapy will work together to heal your heart."

Upon completing her spiel, Dr. Davi stood quietly, presumably waiting for them to make a decision. Delores was the first to speak.

"Um, could we have a little time to consider our options?"

Sharelle's eyes widened. "*What?*" She turned to face her. "*What's there to consider, Mama? She said Dad only has three months to live if we don't do the surgery.*"

"I'll, um..." The cardiologist began to back out of the room. "I'll give you time to consider your options. Take as long as you need. You can have your nurse page me, if I'm no longer on the unit."

When she was gone, Sharelle addressed her mother. "What is there to consider, Mama? Dad needs this surgery."

"Maybe it would be better if we tried the valvuloplasty again," Delores countered.

"We already did that," Sharell said. "It didn't work. That's why he's here now."

"We're also here because his heart disease is progressing. She said it's starting to move to the right side of his heart. She also said even if we have this surgery, he's likely to have other issues within a few years."

"We don't know that for sure."

Delores rolled her eyes slightly.

"Even if it happens," Sharell continued, "that's three years from now. His meds might be working by then. Or we can do another procedure if we have to. If we don't have the surgery, he won't have *any* years left, only a few months. I don't see how this is up for discussion."

She turned to her father, who had been silent while the two women he cared about the most debated his future.

"*Dad, you need to say something*! Don't you want to have this surgery?"

Evan locked eyes with his wife. Her gaze was neutral, but he knew what she wanted to hear. "Your mom's right," he said, returning his attention to his daughter. "What's the point of this surgery, if my heart's gonna give out on me anyway? We already know how this is gonna end. Why are we doing so much to avoid the inevitable?"

Sharelle's eyes grew even larger.

"I didn't say that," Delores quipped.

"*Dad, how could you say that*?" his daughter wailed.

Evan's eyes returned to his wife. Hers were cold and damning.

"Don't put words in my mouth," she told him. "If you feel like it's not worth it, you need to own that."

"So you want my opinion?" he asked her.

"It's your heart," his wife said. "Your opinion is the only one that matters."

He waited a few beats before saying, "I think anything we could do to save my life is worth it. Even if the surgery only adds three years to my life, there's not a price we can put on that. I'll deal with what happens in three years when that time comes."

Delores continued to stare down at him for a few moments before nodding. "Okay then. It's settled. We'll have the surgery."

Sharelle squealed with delight, eager to ignore the marital dynamics that just played out before her. Tears were streaming down her face again.

"Great! I'll go get the doctor!"

"Don't you ever do that again," Delores said when they were alone in the room.

Evan didn't back down. "I only said what you were thinking."

"Even if you *think* that's what I wanted, you have no right to tell our daughter I'm signing your death certificate. I only said we should consider our options. I never said it wasn't worth it, because you're going to die anyway."

Evan felt he'd deciphered her objections accurately, but if she wanted to save face for Sharelle's sake, she deserved an opportunity to do so. He remained quiet for the two minutes it took for his daughter to return with his cardiologist. Likewise, Delores didn't have anything else she wanted to say to him.

"I understand you've decided to go through with the surgery?" Dr. Davi said when she entered the room.

Sharelle was quick on her heels. She looked from one parent to another, as if daring them to change their minds.

"Yes," Evan said. "The valve replacement sounds like the only way I'll have a fighting chance. I wanna keep fighting."

"Good," his cardiologist stated. Then, "You do understand this procedure is not like the ones we've done in the past. This is *open-heart surgery*. The surgeon I'm referring you to will go in through your chest. You will be connected to a ventilator. Your heart will stop beating for a period of time, while he completes the surgery. This is much more risky than the valvuloplasty."

Evan's jaw became unhinged as he stared at her. His wife and daughter must've felt the same dread, because they too were rendered mute.

"It will be alright." Dr. Davi tried to reassure them with a smile. "The surgeon I'm referring you to does amazing work. I have never met a man I admire more..."

CHAPTER SIX
HIPAA

Evan remained at the hospital for three days prior to his surgery. His wife and daughter visited often. Friends from work stopped by as well, but none of their balloons and get well cards were powerful enough to vanquish the sense of dread from his room. The longer he stayed there, the more he came to abhor the smell of disinfectants and the staff's predictable routine. He could set his clock by how often the techs would come to check his vitals and guest services would bring his meals. He even knew the exact moment they would return for his used dishes and ask, "Are you done? You didn't eat much?"

"I wasn't very hungry this morning," he'd reply.

"Dr. Davi wants you to eat more. You need to be strong for your surgery."

"I'll eat more at lunchtime," he'd tell them, and they'd have to leave it at that.

Evan found his loneliness tended to reach its peak during the daytime. With Sharelle at school, his wife at work and his coworkers busy doing his job without his input or expertise, he had little to do but watch TV, peruse the social apps on his phone and think. He was allowed to get out of bed and walk around the unit, but until his surgery, Dr. Davi prohibited him from doing anything too strenuous. Walking to the cafeteria on the first floor of an adjacent building was one of the things that was off limits.

As bad as his cabin fever was, Evan didn't think he'd hate it so much if he wasn't on the first floor.

One afternoon he asked his nurse, "Why am I still in ICU? Do I have to stay in this room until my surgery?"

"Yes," he replied. "Dr. Davi assigned you to this unit."

"But I don't feel like I'm critical," Evan argued. "Do you think she'd be okay with transferring me to C3 for the next couple of days?"

The nurse shook his head. "I know you may not feel critical, but until you get your heart valve replaced, you're at a high risk for a heart attack. This is the appropriate unit for you."

Evan sighed.

"You'd feel more comfortable in Cardiac Telemetry?" his nurse asked.

"Yeah," Evan said with a nod. "I know all the nurses and techs there. I've been on and off that unit for eight years."

"Well," his nurse said, "if it makes you feel any better, after your surgery, you'll spend a few days on the second floor, CVICU, and then you'll be transferred to C3 for the rest of your recovery. You'll probably be there for a week before discharge."

Evan chuckled dryly. "I know that's what I asked for, but the way you put it does not make me feel better. It makes me feel like I'll be at this hospital for fifteen days."

"But most of it will be on C3," his nurse said with a smile.

"Alright," Evan conceded. "I guess that's the best I could hope for. Could you…"

He wanted to ask if his nurse could call upstairs to see if Jada was working that day. He knew she had access to the hospital database, but the system probably wouldn't notify her he was in the cardiac tower until he arrived on her unit.

"What's that?" his nurse asked. "You need me to do something for you?"

Evan wasn't sure what pretense he could use to reach out to his nurse. Contacting Jada just to say hi might blur the line between their patient/caregiver relationship.

"Never mind," he said. "It was nothing."

Delores and Sharelle came later that day. Sharelle brought lemon pepper wings from Wingstop. She knew they were her father's favorite. Delores thought the meal went against his diet. She went as far as going to the nurse' station and checking with his nurse. She seemed a little put-off when she returned and said, "They said you can have it."
Evan gave her a side eye as he chowed down on the wings.

He thought she would be happy that Sharelle found a way to cheer him up.

When their daughter left, Evan welcomed the alone time with his wife. He was past the point of expecting an endearing moment, but he hoped she would open up about how she really felt about the surgery. Initially her responses were supportive, almost dutifully so. He had to ask a leading question to get her going.

"Have you checked with the insurance, to see how much this surgery is going to cost?"

"Yes, I checked." She sat in a recliner next to his bed, browsing through the apps on her cellphone.

Evan waited and then said, "You wanna tell me what they said?"

"Including the anesthesia, it's $86,000."

Evan already knew that number, but he whistled and said, "Damn. That's a grip. How much does our insurance cover?" He knew the answer to this as well. During his time alone in the room, he'd requested a printout from the billing department.

"Your insurance only covers 80 percent. That leaves $17,000 we have to come up with out of pocket."

Evan nodded. "We have eight thousand in savings. Will they take that and put us on another payment plan?"

"They will, but I'm not giving them $8,000. I told them we have four thousand. That'll make our payments higher, but there's no point in being broke and still stuck with a payment plan."

"They agreed to that?"

"Not yet. They're still haggling. They want us to pay at least half."

"We have another thousand in our checking accounts, if we need to give them eighty-five hundred, we can swing it."

She looked up at him. "Evan, I already told you I'm not going to deplete our accounts and still be stuck with a payment plan. That money's for emergencies. What if something happens after this surgery?"

Evan couldn't think of a bigger emergency than a freaking heart attack, but he kept quiet.

"Let me deal with the financial side of this," Delores told him. "That's the least of our worries."

He frowned. "It is?"

She frowned back at him. "You don't think so? After the surgery, what kind of life do you think we'll have? You had a heart attack while mowing the lawn. I know it was hot that day, but it didn't have anything to do with the heat. It's getting to the point where any little activity might put you at risk. Have you thought about what this is going to do to our lifestyle?

"We have to hire someone to cut the grass now – I have no idea where that money is going to come from. Pretty soon it'll get to the point where you can't take out the trash any more or make the bed or maybe even get out of bed. I'm coming to terms with the fact that I may have to take care of you for the rest of my life – or *your* life. Either way, this is not the lifestyle I envisioned for us when we got married. This is not how things are supposed to be."

Evan was devastated to hear her speak like this. He fought hard not to show a reaction.

"Considering all of that," he said, "wouldn't it be better if I don't have this surgery?"

She hmphed at that. "You had time to give that opinion when we first talked to Sharelle about it. Instead you chose to throw me under the bus."

"No, I'm serious. If it comes to the point that I need all of this care, wouldn't it make sense to have our savings and not be on another payment plan? When I can't take out the trash or get out of bed, we'd have enough money to hire someone to take care of me. I wouldn't be a burden on you."

She rolled her eyes. "Evan, it's too late for all of this sound reasoning now. You already let it be known you want this surgery. The conversation we're having is all about money, but I can't put a price tag on the months or years you have left. If you back out now, Sharelle will be devastated. She'll blame me, even if you tell her it was your decision. You're having the surgery. That's the end of that."

Evan continued to stare at her, as her attention returned to her phone. He wondered if he was a glutton for punishment. He already knew how she felt. She didn't give one response that could be considered a revelation. He wasn't sure why he needed her to make it concrete by saying it aloud. Then again, a part of him did need to hear it. Just as all indications made him believe she'd initiate a divorce one day, he wouldn't know for sure until she looked him in the eyes and told him that's what she wanted.

After a few minutes of silence, she stood and said, "Do you need me to stay the night? If so, I have to go home and get my overnight bag."

He shook his head. "No, baby. There's no point of you being stuck in here. I know you have to finish your thesis. It's bad enough I have to be here. No point in both of us suffering."

She nodded as she approached his bed. She bent to kiss him on the lips.

"Alright. I'll come see you tomorrow. I love you."

She didn't notice his eyes gloss over as she backed way.

"Okay, baby," he told her. "You have a good night. I love you too."

The next morning, the day before his surgery, Evan awakened to an empty room once again. He waited until 8 am, before he summoned the courage to make a call he felt unusually awkward about. He wasn't sure why he felt so nervous. After eight years and endless talks, he considered Jada a friend.

As many times as he'd been on the unit, he should've known the number by heart, but he had to call the hospital operator for assistance.

She answered with a bored, "Operator."

"Hi," Evan said. "Could you transfer me to C3?"

"One moment please."

His heart thudded while he waited to be connected. He wasn't sure why he was so nervous. It wasn't like he was calling his side chick. He was reaching out to his nurse publicly. There was nothing untoward about it. But still...

"C3," a male voice answered after a thirty-second hold.

"Hi," Evan said. "Is, is Jada working today?"

"Yes, but I'm not sure where she is. Who's calling?"

Evan's eyes widened. He didn't think they'd ask his name. But then again, why wouldn't they? And why should he feel apprehensive about providing it?

"Evan Shales."

"Okay, could you hold for a moment?"

"Yes. That's fine."

Evan was surprised to find sweat blossoming on his forehead while he waited.

There is nothing wrong with this, he told him himself. *She's been your nurse for eight years. It's okay to tell her you had a heart attack, and you're back in the hospital. It's completely innocent.*

His reassurances did not stop his gut from twisting while he was on hold. After two full minutes, his conscious almost forced him to hang up. But a sweet voice he immediately recognized finally came to the line.

"Hi, this is Jada. Evan?"

The wave of relief and joy that flooded his system felt sinful.

"Hey. Yeah, it's me, Evan. I'm not sure if you know, but I'm in the hospital again. I'm on C1. I, uh, I wanted you to know that I had a heart attack the other day, and I'm having surgery tomorrow."

The extended pause that ensued made him second guess everything. Would he get her in trouble by calling? Did she want to hear from him? Was it against a hospital policy? Was she still upset about the last conversation they had?

After an agonizing five seconds that felt like an hour, she said, "I'm sorry to hear that. Are you okay?"

He sighed. "I am. I mean, I'm not dead, so I guess that's something to be grateful for."

Another pause. Evan didn't have the patience to wait this one out.

"Can you come see me?" he blurted. "I'm in C104. I can understand if you can't, but I'm having surgery tomorrow, and... I know you're not my nurse right now, but if I pull through, I'll be on your floor within a week. You, um... You always make me feel better when I'm at the hospital. I, uh... Shit. I don't... This is stupid. I know you're probably too busy..."

The next pause was only three seconds, but it felt longer than all of the others combined.

She told him, "I think I can stop by later, during my lunch break."

He closed his eyes and took a deep breath. "Okay. I would appreciate that. Thank you."

"Alright," she said. "I'll see you later."

Evan knew Jada's shift started at 6:30 a.m. He guessed her lunch break would be around the midway point. When two o'clock rolled around, and she still hadn't made an appearance, he assumed she had been too busy to get away from her floor. Or maybe she'd changed her mind. The disappointment that ensued was worse than being stuck in ICU. The door to his room remained open throughout the day. At one point, he thought about closing it, so he wouldn't be tempted to look up at every figure walking by.

At 3:45, someone knocked on the door before stepping inside. Evan heard a rustling of balloons before his visitor rounded the corner. His heart leapt when he saw that it was Jada. Her smile and pristine blue scrub suit never looked so good.

"Good afternoon!" She told him. On the way to his bed, she tied the balloons on the bed table with the deftness of someone who had done it hundreds of times. "How you holding up?"

"I'm good," Evan replied. He studied her features, her hair, her soft eyes. Her appearance hadn't changed in the six months since he'd last seen her, but he thought she looked fresh and new.

He told her, "Thanks for coming."

She placed both hands on the bed rail and continued to smile at him. "You know I had to come see my favorite patient."

"I was worried about calling your unit," he revealed. "I didn't know if I'd get you in trouble. I don't know how things work here."

"It's okay for you to call and ask to speak to me. It would be different if you called from home, but you're a patient, so that's okay."

"I wasn't sure if you knew I had gotten admitted."

Her smile slipped a little, and she bit her bottom lip. "Evan, you're right about some of the things you're worried about. I did know you were at the hospital. Dr. Davi told me. She came by to check on some of her patients the other day and told me you'd been admitted to the E.R."

Before Evan asked why she didn't reach out to him, she said, "But knowing someone is a patient here doesn't give me the right to contact them. Even if I heard one of my best friends got admitted, I could get in trouble if I visited them. If they got discharged and didn't tell me they were ever here, I couldn't ask them about it later. That's a HIPAA violation."

Evan had heard about the HIPAA laws, but he didn't know much about them. He knew Jada's knowledge was much more extensive.

"But when you called and invited me to visit you," she said, "that's different. But even with that, I have to be careful. If you were a female patient or elderly, no one would bat an eye. But you're young and handsome, and this hospital is a cesspool of rumors and affairs. People love to gossip. I wouldn't be surprised if some of the nurses on this unit are talking about me right now, even though I brought you balloons."

Evan understood that. He wondered if she brought the balloons to head off any suspicions her coworkers might have. He was also flattered that she thought he was handsome.

"So, how are you feeling about your surgery?"

He shrugged. "It's open heart surgery. Not too much to feel good about."

"You can feel good about getting your valve replaced," she offered. "That's a good thing."

"Yeah, but the doctor said I might have other issues with my heart a few years from now. This surgery will buy me time, but it may not be the end of my troubles."

"Anything can happen in a few years. There are miracles in the world of medicine every day. Like with your heart meds, maybe you're not seeing results with the ones you're taking now. But they could make a new one tomorrow that will cure your heart disease. You gotta stay optimistic."

He grinned. "You're always trying to cheer me up."

She smiled too. "That's my job."

He shook his head. "No, not now it isn't. You're not my nurse at the moment. Everything you're doing is out of the kindness of your heart."

He thought she might have blushed. If her skin tone was a shade lighter, he would've known for sure.

"Jada," he said, "I've been thinking about all you do for me, and I wanted to apologize for what I said the last time I saw you."

She cocked her head. "I don't remember you saying anything you should apologize for."

"When you told me about your divorce, I said '*Then it's not always for better or worse, is it?*'"

She shook her head. "Evan, that was six months ago. Why is that still on your mind?"

He thought for a second. "I guess it's because you've always been so good to me. I don't have many opportunities to return the favor. The one time we talk about something other than me, I said something to hurt you. I'm sorry."

The mood in the room became downcast. Evan would prefer things remained upbeat, but he had to get that off of his chest.

"It's okay," she said. "I know you didn't mean to offend me."

He watched her eyes. Since the tone had already shifted, he decided to probe deeper into the subject. "Is it okay if I ask why you got a divorce?"

She cocked an eyebrow. "Why is that subject so interesting to you?"

"I told you, it's been on my mind recently."

"*My* divorce or divorce in general?"

He maintained eye contact when he replied. "Both."

Jada's eyebrows raised. No way was she going to ask him a follow up question.

"My husband and I divorced because he had an affair," she told him. "Well, multiple affairs, actually. I tried to work it out with him after the first two, but, you know how it goes; you get to a point where you can't work it out anymore."

Evan nodded. "I understand. Do you have kids together?"

"Yes. We have three children."

"Was it hard on them?"

"Yes, of course, but they got through it. We all did. It's not like they were little kids. They understood why I had to leave."

"How long ago was it?"

She hoped this conversation would end soon, but she responded. "It was two years ago. My youngest child was 18 at the time."

After a pause, Evan said, "I don't understand why anyone would cheat on you."

Her smile returned. "That's nice, but you don't know me."

"Are you saying you did something to make him cheat."

Her smile vanished just as quickly. "No. I didn't."

Evan nodded. Unexpectedly, he said, "Another reason I don't want to have the surgery is because I don't want to put my wife in a position to be my caregiver. If I ever get to the point where I have trouble doing little things, like taking out the trash or tying my shoes, I don't think she would be willing to support me."

Jada was trying her best to not discuss Mrs. Shales but that question begged for a response. At that moment, someone entered the room and let her off the hook.

"Hey, Dad."

Sharelle's expression changed when Jada turned to her, and she saw this wasn't her father's nurse from this unit.

"Hi," Jada said. "It's Sharelle, isn't it?"

"Yes. You're my dad's nurse from upstairs, right?"

Jada nodded. "Yes. The last time I saw you, you were a freshman in college. How's school going?"

"It's going great," she said beaming.

"Well, I just came to wish your father luck with his surgery tomorrow – not that he needs it. You're gonna do great," she said to Evan. "I'll let you two be alone. See you guys soon."

"Okay," Evan said. "Thanks for coming."

"Bye," Sharelle told her. When Jada was gone, she turned and eyed her father queerly. "What's she doing here?"

"What do you mean? She's my nurse from C3."

"I know, but you're not on her floor. It's okay for her to come see you like that?"

"Baby girl, she's been my nurse for eight years. You don't think she's invested in my wellbeing, after all this time? Nurses like her is why this hospital is so special. Did you see the balloons she brought me?"

Sharelle looked over at the balloons floating from the bed table. When her eyes returned to her father, she was smiling again.

"That's sweet, Dad. I'm glad she came. It's good to know so many people here care about you."

"I think so too. Now..." He sat up and rubbed his hands together. "What say you smuggle a can of Pringles up in here?"

"Huh? You can't eat Pringles?"

"They got me on a low sodium diet today. The food they've been serving is so bland, all of my taste buds have died."

"Nuh-uh. They ain't gon' do my daddy like that the day before heart surgery. You should be able to have whatever you want. I'll run down to the gift shop."

"Hurry, before your mom gets here. And don't tell her you got them for me."

Sharelle was headed for the door. She looked back at him and smiled. "Okay, Daddy. I won't."

"I love you, baby girl."

"I love you too, Daddy."

CHAPTER SEVEN

UNDER THE KNIFE

The next morning, Evan was surprised by a visit from his family from Washington. He hadn't seen his mother and father in five months. His brother Bennie came too, as well as his Uncle Bill and Aunt Patrice. Seeing his loved ones enter his room brought Evan to tears. Delores was also there with Sharelle, his favorite coworker Jeremy and their boss Gwen.

"Mom, Dad, why didn't you tell me you were coming?"

"We wanted to surprise you."

Evan's mother carried herself with an air of professionalism. She owned two tea shops in the DC area and had recently purchased a third building that was in the process of renovation. Evan always admired the fact that she did all of this without a college degree.

His father also accomplished quite a bit without college. He took a job on a construction site right out of high school. Four decades later, he was the lead foreman for DC's second largest cement company. Both of Evan's parents were considering retirement, but with their drive and work ethics, the thought of not going to work in the morning wasn't appealing, even at their age.

"This is definitely a surprise!" Evan told them. "Mama, I talked to you yesterday. You didn't say anything about going to the airport."

"You know your mama can keep a secret," his father said. "Your wife can too. We're all staying at your house."

That was an even bigger surprise. Delores and Evan's mother hadn't always been on the best terms.

"How are you feeling?" Aunt Patrice asked.

"I'm feeling a lot better now," Evan told her. "I'm really glad y'all came."

She reached and rubbed the top of his head. "You're not scared, are you?"

"A little," Evan admitted.

"I would be too," his father said.

"It's okay to be scared," his mother said.

"I was scared too, when I had my surgery," his uncle chimed in. "But it ain't nothing to it. It's just gon' be like a long nap, and when you wake up, your ticker will be as good as new. You'll be sore for a while, but that'll just give you more time to lay up and relax."

Evan's uncle had heart bypass surgery five years ago, and he healed up just fine. But Uncle Bill didn't know the extent of Evan's heart disease. Evan's ticker wouldn't be as good as new after his surgery. Uncle Bill was also wrong about Evan's desire to lay up and relax. Like his parents, Evan felt useless each day he was unable to go to work.

His nurse entered the room and smiled at all of the people surrounding his bed.

"Whoa! Are we having a party in here?"

They all laughed good-naturedly.

"A tech will be here in a few minutes to take Evan down," she announced. "Do any of you have questions before we wheel him out?"

"How long does the surgery take?" Sharelle asked.

"It will last three to six hours," the nurse told them.

"How long will his heart stop beating?" Sharelle wanted to know.

Evan was surprised his daughter asked. Everyone in the room was quiet as they waited for a response.

"They'll stop his heart for 30 to 90 minutes," his nurse replied. "But don't worry. The heart-lung machine will take over, and his blood will continue to flow like normal. A ventilator will keep him breathing. Everything will be fine. His surgeon has performed hundreds of heart surgeries. Evan is in excellent hands. Do you have any more questions?"

Evan prayed no one else would want details. He'd made the mistake of looking up a valve replacement surgery on YouTube last night. He was already freaked out enough. He didn't need any more details.

Everyone shook their head.

"We don't have any more questions," Evan said. "I'm ready to get to it and get it over with."

"Great," his nurse replied. "When the surgery's over, you'll be transferred to surgical recovery, so they can monitor you as you come out of the anesthesia. After that, you'll be sent to C2 for a few days. I won't be your nurse anymore. I'm a little sad about that, because you've been a great patient! I can see you running a 5K within the next year. When you do, make sure to send me pictures, so I can post them on our bulletin board."

Evan looked around at all of the encouraging faces around him. If any of his friends and family were nervous, they didn't show it. He couldn't remember the last time he felt so loved and so blessed.

"Thank you," he told his nurse. "I've never run a 5K before, but if my heart gets better, that's the first thing I'm gonna do."

"Not *if* it gets better," his mother corrected him. "*When* it gets better."

"That's right," Evan said nodding. "*When* it gets better."

He made the mistake of looking around again until he spotted Delores. Her expression was definitely stuck on *if*, but he didn't let her spoil the mood.

With his eyes, he told her, **When I get better**.

Her lips pursed, as if she understood him completely.

Evan's surgery started at 10 a.m. His group of loved ones left his hospital room and shuffled to the surgery waiting room. The area was large and accommodating, with a coffee machine that also made cappuccinos and expressos. There was also fruit, snacks and three big-screen televisions mounted on the walls. One was tuned into daytime television. Another showed endless news from CSPAN. The third gave updates on the patients currently in surgery. That was the screen Evan's crew gravitated to.

The updates weren't specific. They learned when the surgery officially started and what phase Evan was in. Phase I started when the anesthesia was admitted. Phase II was when they intubated him and connected him to the ventilator. Phase III was when the surgeon made the first incision. Everyone, including Delores, held their breath when the monitor indicated Evan was in Phase III. They knew this phase would last a minimum of three hours, but they couldn't take their eyes off the screen for the first thirty minutes.

Uncle Bill convinced them to take a break.

"Let's go to the cafeteria and get something to eat. He's in God's hands and the surgeon's hands now. We gon' go crazy stressing ourselves out, if we stare at that screen for the next six hours."

Everyone agreed that an anxiety break was in order, everyone except Sharelle. She asked them to bring her something back, but she barely ate when they returned.

Evan reached his sixth and final stage at 2:30. That was when the doctor began to close him up.

"Everything must've gone well," Uncle Bill predicted. "They wouldn't be stitching him closed, if there was still work to do in his heart."

Everyone thought that made sense, but the receptionist in the room wouldn't confirm or deny this.

"The phases are different for each patient," she told them. "If they told you they were closing the breastbone at stage six, I don't have more information. I don't have any information on our patients, other than what's on the screen."

"What the hell is she there for?" Uncle Bill wondered as they walked away from her desk, "to make sure the damn coffee machine is plugged in?"

Any other time, that joke would've killed. But at that moment, it was hard for Evan's group to find humor in anything.

Forty minutes later, they finally got the news they'd been waiting for. The status next to Evan's code number changed from "Stage VI" to "Surgery complete." The words were bold and yellow. Evan's group cheered like their team had just won the Super Bowl.

The waiting room receptionist called them over and said, "Mr. Shales' surgeon will be available to speak with you in about thirty minutes. I'll let you know when he's ready."

"Hell, I guess she ain't completely useless," Uncle Bill said as they walked away.

He got a few chuckles this time.

Evan's surgeon still had sweat on his brow when they called Evan's team back to meet him. They guessed he'd just left the operating room.

He told them, "The surgery went great. I was able to replace Evan's tricuspid valve, and it's functioning properly. I'll give his cardiologist more information about other issues with his heart, and she can share that with you, if Evan consents. But the hard part is done. For a surgery of this magnitude, I'm sure you know the road to recovery will be a lengthy one. It could take six weeks before he starts feeling better and up to six months before he's back to his old self.

"But Evan is young and strong. He may recover sooner. He'll be transferred to C2 when he leaves surgical recovery, and we'll monitor him for a few days before sending him to C3. His cardiologist will have the last word on when he'll be discharged, but I suspect he'll go home in seven to ten days."

All things considered, everyone thought that was great news.

An hour later, they were finally able to see the man of the hour. Evan's new room was C213. He lie flat on his bed, his sheets tucked in tightly. An assortment of IV fluids dripped into tubes that disappeared beneath his sheets. The telemetry monitor mounted above his head displayed six EKG leads. No one in his family could interpret them, but they saw his heart rhythm was mostly normal, and that was all they needed to know.

Evan's face was ashen, his lips chapped. The effort needed to simply keep his eyes open seemed exhausting. He smiled weakly at the same crowd that came to support him at nine o'clock that morning. Since then, none of them had left the hospital.

"I made it," he said. His voice was faint and raspy. He winced at the pain in his throat. He was under anesthesia when they slid an endotracheal tube down his throat before surgery, but he felt the side effects now.

"Yes, you made it," his mother said. She caressed the side of his face. Tears glistened in her eyes.

"How do you feel, Daddy?" Sharelle asked.

He took a deep breath before responding. "Right now... I'm so doped up... I don't feel much. But my chest... It ain't right. I think somebody cut me open..."

His smile was feeble. When the expressions around him remained morose, he said, "That was a joke."

Uncle Bill laughed heartily. "He gon' be alright," he announced. "If you still got a sense of humor after what you been through for the past seven hours, that's a good sign."

Everyone agreed with that. Evan locked eyes with his wife, but he couldn't get a read on what she was thinking. He took solace in the other faces surrounding him.

"I can't wait... to get back to work," he told Gwen.

Even in his inebriated state, he could tell her smile was forced.

"Just worry about getting better," she replied. "That's the important thing."

Evan had to remain on C2 for four days. On day one, his cardiologist came with good and bad news.

"Your surgery went great. Your heart is adapting well to your artificial valve. Your blood is flowing as it should. But Dr. Chen noticed things we can't see as well on the ECHO. The progression of your heart disease is worrisome. Dr. Chen recommended we change one of your medications, and I agree with him. We'll keep trying, until we find the combination of medications that gets you better. In the meantime, we'll focus on recovering from surgery. How's your chest feeling?"

"It hurts, doc," Evan said honestly. "I looked at the scar when they were changing my dressing. It's weird, knowing they split my chest open like that."

"Pain at the incision site is to be expected. Would you like for me to up your pain medication?"

"No. I already feel doped up half the day. It hurts, but it's manageable. I'll be alright."

On day two, Evan felt well enough to hug and kiss his family from Washington before they headed home. He appreciated the support they had given him, and though he didn't want them to go, he understood they had obligations they needed to attend to.

"Thanks again for coming," he told them. "Y'all don't know how much that meant to me."

With his Washington family gone, Evan's visits withered down to just Delores, Sharelle and a few friends who popped in occasionally. His daughter was out of school for the summer, but Evan would not allow her to spend more than three hours in his room on any day.

"Baby girl, I love you, but you gotta go," he'd tell her. "The weather is beautiful outside. I don't want you cooped up in here."

"But Daddy–"

"No, I'm serious. Go to a water park. Go downtown. Go shopping. I don't care what you do, but you gotta get out of here."

She sighed and pouted, but eventually she'd comply.

Evan's visits with his wife gradually became more of a stressor than a blessing. It was clear she was resentful, both of his surgery and the recovery process. He no longer needed her to vocalize her grievances. He actually preferred when she worked on her laptop or stared at her phone and didn't speak to him at all.

On day three, Jada surprised him with a visit. Evan hadn't had much to smile about that day, but his face lit up when she walked into his room with more balloons.

"There's my favorite patient!"

"Hey, Jada!"

He winced when he tried to sit up too quickly. She let go of the balloons and rushed to his bedside. She placed a hand on his shoulder.

"Evan, lie back down. Don't try to sit up. What are you thinking?"

"Sorry," he said, gasping slightly. "I got a little excited."

"You're gonna give *me* a heart attack, trying something like that."

Evan knew it was wrong to relish the way she patted his shoulder, but he couldn't help it. Her touch was so tender, so caring.

"Well," she said, withdrawing her hand. "I heard your surgery went great! How do you feel, other than not being able to sit up?"

"I'm okay," he told her. "I'm sore, but I guess that's to be expected."

"Yes, it is. Open heart surgery is no easy thing."

"It's not, but I'm good. Did Dr. Davi tell you what the surgeon said about my heart?"

She shook her head. "No, other than the surgery was a success."

"Dr. Chen said my heart disease is progressing. He could get a better look at it than Dr. Davi, when he opened me up."

"We're not gonna let that get us down," Jada said quickly, a little too quickly. Evan wondered if she was already aware of that before he told her. "Our focus right now is you recovering from surgery. We'll continue to work on your heart disease along the way."

Evan chuckled. "You sound like my doctor."

"All of your caregivers are on one accord," she told him. "We all want you to get better as soon as possible. How are you feeling mentally?" she asked. "You know you have to maintain optimism for any of this to work."

"I'm trying," he said. "When I had my surgery, my family from Washington was here. I had a lot of loved ones around me. But when it was over, and it got down to just me and my wife, that's when depression started to set in. I don't think things are gonna get better with us."

"I'm sorry to hear that." Her eyes and tone expressed true concern. "I hope you're wrong, and the two of you can work it out. In the next few months, you'll need her more than ever."

"Yeah," he said with a grunt. "That's what I'm afraid of."

She didn't say anything.

"Can I ask about your divorce again?"

Jada didn't like discussing that, but she didn't like talking about his marital problems even more. She nodded. "What do you want to know, Evan?"

"How long were you married?"

She sighed. "We were married for 24 years."

His eyes widened. "Wow. That's a long time."

Her nostrils flared when she took her next inhalation. "Yeah. It is."

"Was it hard to leave him, after all that time?"

She nodded. "I'd been with him for half my life. It was the hardest thing I've ever done."

"Do you still love him?"

She shook her head. "No, but I did when we got divorced. That's one of the reasons I waited so long."

"You said he cheated on you..."

She nodded.

He waited.

She sighed again. "In one year's time, he had three affairs. The first two were going on at the same time. I don't know how he managed to juggle three women, but he did, for almost six months."

"How'd you find out?"

"I had my suspicions. You know what they say; *A woman knows*. I confronted him. He lied. I showed up at his job one day and followed him."

Evan raised an eyebrow.

"I had to know for sure," she said, her features hard, her eyes steely. "I followed him straight to another woman's house. Caught him red-handed. When we got home, he admitted to everything. He swore he would never do it again. I wanted to believe him. I tried so hard to trust him again, but I – I just couldn't. I would say our marriage was over at that point. If you don't trust your husband to work late or go hang out with his friends, it's hard to have a normal relationship.

"When I caught him again six months later..." She shook his head. "I knew things could never go back to the way they were. I think he was having a midlife crisis, but that's no excuse. That's no reason to rip our family apart. But let him tell it, I'm the one who ripped the family apart by filing for divorce. He had the nerve to try to get me back for leaving him.

"He contested everything, from the house to the savings to my 401K. Our divorce dragged on for a year and a half. By the time it was over, I hated him. But I don't hate him anymore. I've forgiven him, but I'll never forget what he did to me, to our family. We had to sell the house and split the equity. I had to start my life over. I'm better now, got everything back on track."

Evan had been listening intently, fully enthralled in the gravity of her story. When she was done, he was at a loss for words. He said, "I'm sorry you had to go through that," but that felt wholly inadequate.

"It's okay," she said, returning to her old self. "I'm hoping now that you've gotten all the details, you can let that story die. I don't like talking about it."

"I know you don't."

"Really?" she said with a grin. "I can't tell, the way you keep bringing it up."

"I asked about it because I'm starting to wonder if divorce might be a viable option for me."

Her smile disappeared. "I know, Evan."

"When I bring up Delores, you never say anything," he noticed. "You've got plenty of good advice, but never about her."

She shook her head. "No. I think it's improper – not because I'm your nurse, but because I don't want to say anything that would sway you one way or the other."

He nodded. "That's understandable."

His heart dropped when she checked her watch. She noticed his reaction to the move.

"You don't want me to leave," she guessed.

He shook his head.

"I'm sorry, but I have to. I gotta get back to work, and I already told you about the gossips here. They know it doesn't take this long to congratulate someone for making it through surgery."

"Okay, well, you'd better go then."

She reached and touched his hand. She stared down at him for so long, Evan wondered if she was contemplating kissing him.

Instead she said, "I'll see you later," barely above a whisper, and walked out of the room.

CHAPTER EIGHT

HOME AWAY FROM HOME

Evan had been anxious to be transferred to C3 since he arrived in ICU. His anxiety reached its peak on his fourth day on C2.

When Dr. Davi came to check on him, he asked her, "Is there a milestone you're waiting for me to reach, before I can get transferred off this unit?"

She smiled. "Why do you ask, Evan?"

"You know I hate it here. I think I hate this floor more than I hate C1."

"All heart surgery patients have to recover on CVICU," she explained. "I don't think I could get around that if I wanted to. But for the record, I don't want to. The nurses on this floor are specialized."

"I get it. I was just wondering if there was something I could do, like walk a mile or something, that would let you know I'm well enough to leave ICU."

She laughed. "Evan, if you could walk a mile, I'd discharge you altogether. But I don't want you to try that. Today's your last day on this unit. You've already made it past the ICU observation threshold, and your incision site is healing properly. I'll transfer you to C3 in the morning."

Evan smiled at that. "Great. Thanks, doc."

Evan had three visitors that day. The first was a surprise. His manager Gwen popped in at lunchtime with a card that had been signed by everyone in their department.

"Thank you! This is awesome," Evan said as he read it. "I really miss y'all."

"We miss you too. How's your recovery going?"

"Doc says I'm doing fine. She's going to transfer me out of ICU tomorrow."

"That's great news, Evan!"

"I was wondering, do you think it would be alright to get back to work when I move upstairs? I could work on my laptop and skype with Jeremy."

She frowned at that. "I'm okay with you working remotely, but how about we wait till you're out of the hospital? I'm pretty sure your doctor would rather you devote your time to getting better."

"What if I get a note from her that says it's okay?"

"You're really persistent."

"I'm going a little stir crazy, with nothing to do all day."

"I understand. If you get a note from your doctor, I'll see what we can do."

"Thanks a lot," he said, his smile brightening. "That would be awesome."

Sharelle came by later with news Evan wasn't so glad to hear.

"Earl asked me to marry him."

Her grin was ear to ear, while Evan's smile turned upside down. Earl was her boyfriend of two years. Evan had only met him half a dozen times.

Noticing his expression, she said, "I knew you wouldn't be happy to hear that."

"Are you sure you knew that, because you seemed pretty excited to tell me."

"What do you have against Earl?"

"Well, first off, what kind of name is *Earl*? That's not much of a name. It only has four letters."

She laughed. "Your name only has four letters, Dad."

"Yeah, but *Evan* is *majestic*. It didn't take any effort to come up with a name like *Earl*. Nothing intriguing about that name at all."

"So, you don't want me to marry him because you don't like his name?"

He grunted. "No, it's not that baby girl. I don't want you to get married because you're a junior in college. You've got a whole lot of living to do. You wanna get locked down while you're still in college?"

"First of all, we would wait until after graduation before we got married. And Dad, I'm 21. Didn't you marry Mom when you were 21?"

He grunted again. Why did she have to be so rational? And bringing up Delores didn't help her argument. But Sharelle didn't know her parents were no longer a match made in heaven.

"Isn't he supposed to come to me first?" he asked. "I know times have changed, but don't guys still ask the father for their daughter's hand in marriage?"

"He wanted to come," she said, "but I didn't know if it was a good idea, with you being in the hospital. If you got upset, and something started to go wrong with your heart..."

Evan didn't think the boy would upset him enough to have another heart attack, but he appreciated his daughter looking out for him. He looked her in the eyes and realized he was raining on her parade. He wanted her to continue living her life to the fullest, and not worry so much about him. Her engagement might serve as a suitable distraction.

"Okay," he said. "But if this guy's serious, you need to bring him to the hospital to talk to me. I promise I won't blow a fuse."

"Really? Thanks Dad!"

She bent over the bed and hugged him tightly. She withdrew just as quickly.

"*Oh my God*! Did I hurt you? I'm sorry. Are you okay?"

"I'm fine," he said, though the pain in his chest had spiked. "I'm not as fragile as you think," he lied.

Delores stopped by after work. She was busy on her laptop for most of the visit. She was more engaged with his nurse, when she stopped by. Delores wanted to know how long Evan would be in the hospital, how long his recovery would last when he got home, and what sort of tasks he'd be able to do once there. Evan lie quietly and angrily while his wife assessed his level of incompetence.

When the nurse left his room, he couldn't stop himself from asking, "Do you love me?"

She frowned at him. "What kind of question is that?"

"The kind of question you didn't answer," he shot back.

"Of course I love you, Evan. Why are you asking me that?"

He answered her with another question. "Would you say your career is your number one priority?"

She continued to frown. "Do you mean right now, or are you asking if I've always felt that way?"

"I would like to know if you've always felt that way, but I was talking about now."

"I think right now it has to be," she replied. "You know your medical bills are piling up. I don't know how much you'll be able to help when you get out of the hospital. If I have to carry us, making my career a priority is necessary. I'm working hard for the both of us."

"None of that is an expression of true love," he countered.

"What do you mean? I just said everything I'm doing is for you. I'll make sure you're taken care of, Evan. If it comes to the point where I have to hire a nurse to care for you, I'll take care of it. If I didn't love you, I wouldn't offer to do any of this. I'd much rather buy a new car or a new home, but if that money has to go to your medical needs, then so be it. You can accuse me of a lot of things, but don't say I don't love you. Obviously, you're the one who doesn't know what love is."

Her voice became more shrill during her spiel. She wasn't yelling, but it was enough to make a passing PCT pause and glance into the room.

Delores shot to her feet unexpectedly. "You know what, I'm not feeling this right now."

Evan's tone was the opposite of hers. He calmly asked, "You're not feeling this hospital or me?"

"Both. Is there anything you need me to do for you before I head home?"

He shook his head.

She approached the bed and bent to kiss him on the lips. "I'll see you tomorrow."

The next morning, Evan was elated when a transporter entered his room and announced he was taking him upstairs. Rather than a wheelchair, he pushed his whole bed out of the room, down the hallway and onto a staff elevator. When they emerged on C3, Evan spotted Jada at the nurses' station. She noticed him too and waved.

"Hey, Evan."

"Morning," he said as the transporter wheeled by her. "I'm back."

"Yes, you are! I'll come check on you in a few minutes," she told him and turned back to the nurse she was speaking to.

Evan's new room, for presumably the next 6 to 7 days was C322. He didn't think he'd ever been in that room before, but all of the rooms on the floor were identical. The feeling of nostalgia was bittersweet. More than anything, he wanted to go home, but this was the next best thing.

Jada stopped by thirty minutes later. Evan was so happy to have her near him, his heart sighed.

"Morning," he said.

"Good morning, Evan. You finally made it."

"Yes, I made it. I'm so glad to be here."

"Me too."

They watched each other's eyes and smiled.

"You didn't tell me I was your favorite patient," Evan noticed.

She stepped closer to his bed, still grinning. "You know you're my favorite patient. You need to hear it every time?"

"No, but I do like to hear it."

She chuckled. "Evan, you are my favorite patient in the whole, wide world."

Watching her lips as she spoke made his body flush with heat.

"And you're my absolute favorite nurse," he replied.

This time he was sure she blushed.

"I wanted to apologize for something," she said.

"What's that?"

"For not hearing you out when you wanted to talk to me about the troubles you're having. I consider you a friend. We've talked about everything through the years. If you want to talk to me about your problems, I'll listen. But I won't offer any advice on your marriage. Deal?"

His eyes were serious when he nodded. "Deal."

Jada heard the sound of a portable computer behind her a second before a PCT rolled it into the room. The techs always came to take a patient's initial vitals within an hour of them arriving on a new unit. Today was no exception.

"I'll be back later," Jada told Evan. "Try to get some rest. Dr. Davi has some physical therapy lined up for you."

"Okay," he said.

The tech watched his eyes follow Jada out of the room. She looked back at the nurse and then back to the patient. Her brow furrowed. Her eyes remained narrowed as she approached the bed.

"Morning, Mr. Shales. I'm Trisha. I'll be your tech for the day shift."

"Hi, Trisha," Evan said. "I think I've seen you before. I've been on this unit a million times..."

True to her word, Jada returned to his room after lunchtime – not to discuss Evan's therapy schedule, but to listen to what he had to say about his wife. Evan was eager to open up to her. Towards the end of their talk, Jada's stomach was a bundle of nerves.

"At this point," he was saying, "I don't know what to think. She's always put her career first, but she's doing it more now. I used to find her drive so attractive. But for the past few years, it has started to drive a wedge between us. You said this was a time when I'd need her the most. I believe that's true. But this is also a time when she can't give me what I need."

"What do you feel you need that she's not providing?" Jada wondered.

"Attention would be a start," he said. "It would be nice if she came to visit me and didn't spend most of her time on her laptop or iPhone. I need to know that she loves me. She says she does, but her actions don't show it. All she does is complain about the medical bills and how me being sick is ruining her fairytale ending. She tells me all the time that this is not how she expected our lives to go.

"That's why I keep telling you I don't want to be a burden on her," he said. "I think it would be different if I needed her and she wanted to be there for me. But that's not the wife I have. I need her, and she makes it clear that she doesn't want to do the things she has to do for me. At this point, I feel like if I have to leave this hospital alone, in a wheelchair or whatever, I'd be better off dealing with my condition on my own, than having to worry about my heart and how much my wife hates me."

Jada inhaled sharply. It took every bit of willpower to keep her glossy eyes from spilling.

"So, that's it," he said. "I know you said you wouldn't offer me any advice. And I respect that. But I'm really glad you took the time to listen. The things I told you, I haven't said to anyone else. It was, I really needed to get that off my chest."

Jada nodded. "Okay, Evan. I'm sorry for what you're going through. I do feel a certain kind of way about what you said, but I have to keep those thoughts in my heart, for now at least. If you ever want to talk, about anything, I'll always be here to listen."

He nodded. "Thank you. I really appreciate that."

She checked her watch. Evan knew he'd been speaking to her for more than twenty minutes. He tried not to show his disappointment, but she saw through him.

She said, "You don't want me to go?"

He shook his head. "No, but I don't want to get you in trouble. I understand you can't spend too much time with me. I'll take whatever I can get – and be grateful for it."

He smiled. She did too.

"I'll check on you again before the end of my shift," she promised.

"Okay," he said. "I can't wait."

CHAPTER NINE

HERE COMES THE BRIDE

When Jada returned to the nurses' station, one of the techs asked if she could speak to her.

"Sure, what's up?"

"Come over here," Trisha said, leading her away. "I wanna show you something."

Jada followed her friend from the nurses' station. She became confused when she led her into an empty patient room.

"What's going on?" Jada asked.

Trisha looked past her to make sure no one had followed.

"What's going on with you and 22?" she asked in a hushed voice, referring to Evan by his room number.

Jada thought she'd been careful, but she wasn't surprised the question was raised.

"Nothing," she said, her eyebrows bunched. "What do you mean?"

"Y'all don't have something going on?"

Trisha was short and full-figured. Jada had worked with her since Trisha was hired on the unit five years ago. They had a good relationship. They never hung out outside of work, but on the floor, Jada considered her a friend and confidant.

"No," she said. "We don't have anything going on. Why would you ask me that?"

"You were talking to him about something earlier," Trisha said, "and y'all cut it short when I came in. And I saw the way he was looking at you. Y'all don't like each other?"

Jada shook her head. "Girl, no. We were talking about some personal things he has going on, but it had nothing to do with us liking each other."

"You can tell me, Jada. I know what I saw when he was looking at you. Maybe you don't like him, but he definitely likes you."

Jada wasn't surprised to hear that. "Well, if he does, he never said anything like that. You know he's married."

"That don't mean nothing. Half the people sleeping with each other around here are married."

Jada continued to shake her head. "Evan's not like that. And you know I'm not."

"I know girl. You one of few people in this hospital with a squeaky-clean reputation. I just wanted to let you know people are talking."

Jada's nostrils flared. "People like who?"

"Some people on C2 said you went to visit him. They said you went and saw him on C1 too."

Jada shook her head, grinning. She didn't like the idea of accusations about her spreading around the hospital, but she was glad it was something she could easily explain.

"I've been 22's nurse for eight years. He had a heart attack, and he had to have heart surgery. He called the floor and told me where he was and asked if I could stop by. I visited him again after the surgery, to see how he was doing.

I know the people up here love to talk, but they doing a little too much right now. A nurse can't visit a patient on another floor? Damn. Don't they have anything better to do than keep tabs on who visits who?"

Trisha chuckled at that. "Girl, you know they don't. I was just letting you know people are watching y'all. If it ain't nothing to it, I wouldn't worry about it."

"I'm not worried about it," Jada said. "Not at all."

"Hey, another thing," Trisha said. "I need to give 5 a bath. Last time I was in there by myself, he grabbed my titty. Can you help me bathe him?"

Jada laughed. She'd heard the old fogey in 305 was a horndog. He also had dementia, so the staff had to give him a pass on some of his undesirable behaviors.

"Yeah. I'll help you with his frisky ass."

Just before shift change, Jada was a little chagrined to see Evan's wife arrive on the unit. She checked herself, wondering why a visit from Evan's wife bothered her. On a carnal level, she couldn't rule out jealousy. But Jada thought her feelings were more tied to her need to care for her patient. If Evan had negative feelings about his wife, it could have an impact on his health. There was nothing wrong with his nurse being concerned about that.

Twenty minutes later, it appeared her worries may have been warranted. The monitor tech on the unit noticed an elevated heart rate in C322.

"Hey, Jada," he called. "22's rate just went from 65 to 90."

Typically, a patient's heart rate wasn't cause for concern until it reached 120 or higher. But given Evan's recent surgery, his alarm control had been lowered to 100. Jada approached the tech and looked over his shoulder.

"Have you ever seen it this high?"

The tech shook his head. "Highest I've ever seen for him is mid 70's."

The charge nurse came to see what they were looking at.

"Who is that," she asked, "the new patient?"

"Yeah," Jada said. "He just had surgery four days ago."

"You wanna check on him?" she asked. Her name was Sheila. She'd been on the unit for over a decade. She was easy to get along with, but when she cracked down on something or someone, no one wanted to be in her crosshairs.

"I can," Jada said, "but I think his wife is in there with him."

"Yeah, I saw her go in there a few minutes ago," Trisha said.

Jada looked back, surprised Evan's cardiac event had drawn such a crowd. There were now four people watching his heart rhythm.

"I'ma go check to see if they got the door closed," Trisha said. She returned a few moments later with a grin. "Yeah, it's closed," she announced. "Is it still high?"

"We're up to 94," the monitor tech said.

"Him and his wife prolly getting busy," Trisha deduced.

That possibility made Jada's heart drop. There was no denying it was jealousy this time.

It was not uncommon for patients to become intimate with their spouse or significant other while in the hospital. As far as the staff was concerned, it was frowned upon but not a cause to put someone out. Normally the couple would be let off with a warning, or multiple warnings. In the worst-case Jada was aware of, administrators had to get involved when a tech walked into a patient's room and found him on top of his wife an unprecedented 4th time. Even in that instance, the remedy they settled on was for all staff to knock on the patient's door before entering.

The contents of Jada's stomach did flips, while they watched Evan's heart rate steadily increase. When it hit 100, the charge nurse asked, "At what rate did Dr. Davi say we need to check on the patient?"

"A hundred," Jada said stoically. Her heart rate was increasing as well. The thought of Evan making love to his wife was troubling enough. The fact that he would do it a week after heart surgery was irresponsible.

Jada knew it was wrong to feel betrayed, but she couldn't help it. Evan had poured out his heart to her, just a few hours ago. He said his wife hated him, and he was contemplating leaving her. How could they have made up so quickly? Even if they had, makeup sex at the hospital was rachet. She thought she knew him better.

"I think we should check on him," Sheila said.

Jada's heart thudded. No way did she want any parts of that. It was bad enough she knew it was happening. She definitely didn't want to see it.

"We, I don't want to interrupt them," she said. "It's um, I mean, it's bad, but they are married."

"And he's your patient," Sheila countered. "I thought you said Dr. Davi set the parameters."

Jada couldn't get her thoughts together.

"She did, but they have to sustain, don't they?"

The monitor tech nodded. "I don't have to contact a nurse unless they sustain for more than five minutes. His heart rate has only been over a hundred for about thirty seconds."

But it rose to the 110's in the next few seconds.

"Okay, we should go," Jada said, volunteering her charge to go with her.

"You don't think you can handle this alone?"

"I don't want to," Jada said.

"I'ma go too," Trisha piped in.

Jada knew her coworker was a notorious gossip. Trisha wanted all the dirt on Evan's illicit activities. Jada, on the other hand, didn't want to go to room 322 at all, so the more the merrier.

The trio rounded the corner and approached Evan's room. They gathered suspicious stares from other employees on the unit. When they reached his door, Jada was relieved and also horrified to hear loud voices coming from inside. Sheila's mouth fell open. Jada didn't mind when her charge took the lead and barged into the room.

They found Delores standing over the bed, her finger in Evan's face. He was sitting up, bracing himself with strong, stiff arms. He was so angry, the veins bulged in his face and neck. Sweat glistened on his forehead.

"*What do you expect me to do?*" he growled. "*Walk out of here right now?!*"

"*If you was half the man–*"

Sheila cut Delores off. The charge nurse's eyes were wide and filled with indignation. But even in her state of alarm, she managed to maintain decorum.

"*What in the heck is going on in here?*"

Delores spun on her, her finger still in Evan's face.

"What's it to you? This is a private conversation between me and my husband! You can't run in here like that!"

"Yes I can!" Sheila shot back. "He may be *your* husband, but he's *my* patient. I can't have you coming in here causing his heart rate to increase like this. I need you to step out of the room."

When Delores didn't get moving quickly enough, she brought the bulldog out of the charge nurse.

"*Now!*" Sheila barked.

Delores was used to being the one giving orders at her job, but she was on someone else's turf now. Stunned, she recoiled and came to her senses as she took in all the people in the room. She snarled as she stormed pass them.

Jada stood frozen in place. She wanted to run to Evan's side, but her charge nurse was still stuck on grizzly mode.

"You need to go talk to her!" she yelled at Jada.

Jada left the room, walking on pins and needles. In her 24 years of nursing, she'd been charged with reprimanding countless hospital visitors. But she felt personally vested this time. With her feelings for Evan and all he'd told her about Delores, she didn't think she could speak to the woman objectively.

She found Evan's wife brewing outside the room. Delores stood with her arms folded over her chest. Jada's apprehension left her as she stared at the woman Evan swore to have and to hold, till death did them part. Delores didn't appear to have any regrets for what just happened. Jada's anger rose as she recalled everything Evan had told her earlier that day and considered what this woman was still doing to harm him, while he was at his most vulnerable.

"I know you know better than to be arguing with your husband while he's in the hospital."

"We weren't arguing," Delores snapped.

"We heard you from outside the door," Jada snapped back. "And we've been watching Evan's heart rate. You got him all the way to 109. You know you can't get him upset right now. What are you trying to do, kill him?" Her face was set in a sneer. She didn't realize that she had stepped within three feet of Delores' personal space.

"You need to get up out my face." Delores' mug was set in a sneer as well.

"*Or what?*" Jada roared. With her eyes glued on Delores', she didn't see the woman's slapping hand stiffen. But she sensed it. "Try it," she dared her. "I'll have you arrested, and you won't see your husband till you get out of jail, and he gets discharged."

Delores considered her options and apparently came to the conclusion Jada knew she would. As good as it might feel to slap the shit out of Evan's nurse, the ramifications of getting arrested for assault would derail the amazing career she was working so hard to obtain.

Instead she opted for verbal aggression.

"Fuck you," she said and stormed back into Evan's room.

Jada was quick on her heels.

"Wait, you can't–"

By the time she caught up with her, Delores had snatched her purse from the chair and was on her way back out. She charged at Jada so aggressively, she flinched as she moved out of the way. But Delores didn't lay a hand on her. She marched down the hallway, past a slew of gawkers, and had to wait nearly a minute for an elevator to arrive on the floor. Delores kept her face forward the whole time, refusing to look back at the many people she knew were staring at her.

Jada wanted to talk to Evan alone after his wife left, but the charge nurse was still in his room. After calming him down and checking to see if he ripped any of his sutures during the outburst, Sheila continued to lead the de-escalation.

"Mr. Shales, you know you're in no condition to be arguing like that, with anyone."

"I'm sorry," Evan said. He was back to his old self, his response almost sheepish.

Jada checked the monitor over his bed. In the three minutes since Delores had left, his heart rate was down to a smooth 82.

"But it wasn't my fault," he argued. "She just gets me so..." He shook his head.

"Well, when I came in here, I saw you ready to hop out of bed," Sheila said. "And you were yelling back at her as much as she was yelling at you. It takes two to tango, you know."

Jada wished she was having this talk with him – alone. Sheila didn't know Evan and Delores' history. She was sure that whatever happened to get Evan to the point they saw him in, Delores was at fault. Then again, Sheila had a point. Just because someone triggers you, doesn't mean you have to have such a strong reaction.

Evan must have felt the same way. He said, "You're right. I shouldn't have let her get to me."

"Do we need to ban her from visiting you, for the rest of the time you're here?" Sheila proposed.

Jada hoped he'd say yes, but Evan shook his head.

"No. She's my wife. If she wants to visit me, I'm okay with it."

"Okay," Sheila said. "It's your decision – unless we have another incident like tonight. If it happens again, it'll be out of your hands. Do you understand?"

He nodded. "I won't let anything like that happen again," he promised.

He locked eyes with Jada, who was standing at her charge nurse's side. She could tell he wanted to talk to her about what happened. They both wished they could be alone in the room.

Unfortunately, that moment would have to wait.

When they got back to the nurses' station, Jada saw that her nighttime relief was already there, waiting for her to give report. As expected, the station was abuzz with the latest gossip. Trisha had told everyone about the commotion in 22. Jada's relief, a redhead named Natalie, wasn't interested in much of what Jada had to say about the other patients she was handing off to her. She only wanted to hear about Evan.

"I heard you went off on his wife."

Jada didn't want to be part of the rumor mill. She was mentally drained. What she wanted most was to return to Evan's room and make sure he was okay. But she had no cause to do so at the moment, especially since his nightshift nurse had arrived. The only other thing she wanted was to go home.

"I did get upset with her," she acknowledged. "It pissed me off to see her arguing with him." She thought about the speculations the staff on C1 and C2 had started and added, "Both of them were acting like fools."

Natalie laughed. "That's crazy. Mr. Half Dead should know better."

Jada chose not to react to that, but she asked, "*Mr. Half Dead?*"

"Yeah, that's what we call him on night shift. I forget who started it, but that was back when he had 50% heart function. He's worse than that now. We should probably start calling him Mr. Three-Quarters Dead." She chuckled at her own joke.

It hurt Jada to know people were talking about Evan like that, but she learned two things. First, whatever rumors there might be at the hospital about her and Evan couldn't have been too serious or widespread, or Natalie never would've said that to her. Second, some of the nurses at the hospital failed to treat patients with the compassion and dignity they deserved, which was part of the hospital's mission statement.

"Y'all crazy," she said, forcing her lips to curve into a smile. "Well, I'll see you and 22 next week. I got the next four off."

"Ooh girl, that's a blessing!" Natalie said. "Enjoy yourself."

Jada smiled and nodded before walking away. Any other time, four days off in a row was a blessing. Tonight, it almost felt like a curse.

CHAPTER TEN

FLORENCE NIGHTINGALE

Jada couldn't make it through one day away from work before her nerves started to get the best of her. Being away from the hospital meant she was completely cut off from Evan. He was the first thing on her mind when she woke up. She wondered what his heart rate was currently, and if it had remained stable overnight. She wondered if his wife had a change of heart by the time Delores made it home last night. Did she call Evan to apologize? Did he forgive her?

The look in his eyes the last time Jada saw him weighed heavily on her soul. She knew he was anxious to talk to her. Did he want to explain what had led him and his wife to have such a heated argument, or did he have more consequential news? Maybe he'd decided to leave Delores. Could that be what they were arguing about?

Jada had told him she hoped everything worked out with his marriage. At the time, she believed she had meant it. She no longer felt that way. Evan deserved better. She wouldn't be surprised if everyone who knew the couple felt that way.

By noon that day, Jada knew she was headed off the deep end when she considered calling her unit to check on him. If she pulled that move, the rumors that were swirling around C1 and C2 would seem miniscule compared to the suspicious stares she'd encounter when she returned to work in a few days.

To get her mind off things, she called an old friend and invited her to lunch. That didn't help. Before their meal arrived, Jada's troubled patient monopolized their conversation.

"I keep thinking about what his night shift nurse said," Jada confided. "She called him Mr. Half Dead."

"*Mr. Half Dead?*" Brenda looked as offended as Jada had felt last night.

The ladies once worked together in the Meredith building at Jackson Memorial, before Jada transferred to C3, and her friend moved to Dallas. Brenda now worked as a cardiac nurse at Parkland.

Jada nodded. "Yep. That's what she said. She said that's what the night shift staff called him."

"That's some cold-hearted shit," Brenda said. "Nurses like that, they not gon' know what it feels like till something happens to them. When they're laid up in a hospital bed, karma gon' come back at them."

Jada nodded. "The thing is, Evan does have a lot of heart issues. Today I was wondering what would happen if by the time I get back to work, I find out he passed away." The mere thought caused a sick sensation to roll down her frame.

"I was thinking," Jada went on, "how they wouldn't call to let me know something had happened. I've lost patients before when I was off work. You know how it is."

Brenda nodded. "Yeah, it just happened to me last month. I was only off for one day. When I went back, one of my patients' rooms was empty. I thought he got discharged, but when I asked about him, they told me he had died."

Jada swallowed roughly. The waiter brought their food. It was one of Jada's favorite dishes, but that afternoon, it looked disgusting. Her friend studied her demeanor.

"What'd you say this patient's name was?"

"Evan."

"Eight years is a long time to be someone's nurse," her friend said. "Is he a frequent flyer?"

"I usually see him two to three times a year."

"Are y'all close enough to exchange numbers?" Brenda wanted to know.

Jada shook her head but said, "I mean, we are. I don't know. Either way, we wouldn't, because he's married."

"But if you did, you wouldn't be so worried about him. You could just call him to see if he's alright."

Jada considered that. She shook her head. "I don't think I'd be able to do it. I'd be too worried about who's in the room with him. He wouldn't be able to talk to me if his wife was there. I don't want that kinda drama in my life."

Brenda continued to watch her.

"What?" Jada asked.

"I didn't say nothing."

"You're staring at me like you want to say something."

"I'm just wondering about your relationship with him. I know you said he's married, but do you have feelings for him?"

Jada shook her head. "Not like you're thinking."

"Is there more than one way to have feelings for someone?"

"Brenda, I care for him, more than I have ever cared for a patient. But that's where it ends. The things he's gone through, what he's still going through. You know how sometimes you'll hear about someone who was dealt a bad hand in life, and they're such a good person, it breaks your heart because they don't deserve it. I think this is the first time I've ever known someone like that personally."

"So this *concern* you have is all about sympathy?" Brenda asked.

Jada nodded. "Yeah. That's all it is." She frowned, considering how often she was lying to people who would probably be understanding if she was honest with them. This new character trait she had developed wasn't something she was comfortable with.

Brenda's eyes narrowed.

Jada sighed. Unexpectedly, her eyes filled with tears. Her friend reached across the table and took her hand.

"Girl, what's wrong?"

"I don't – I'm sorry I'm lying to you."

Brenda nodded. "It's alright. Do you wanna tell me what's going on? You can talk to me."

Jada shook her head but said, "I think I'm in love with that man."

Her friend didn't register the shock Jada had expected.

She asked, "How long have you felt this way?"

"I don't know," Jada said, her features contorted in uncertainty. "Over a year, at least."

Brenda's eyes widened slightly. "That's a long time. Does he know how you feel? Have y'all talked about it?"

"No. I think he feels the same way, but he's never said it."

"Then how do you know?"

"I've known him for so long," Jada explained. "We talk about everything. I know when he's up. I know when he's down. I've been there through all his emotions. Lately he's been upset because of what's going on with his wife. He's not happy with her. I feel helpless, because I'm trying to do the right thing and tell him to work it out. But I just... Deep down, I don't want him to stay with her. I know it's wrong for me to feel that way, especially after what happened with me and Karl."

Brenda was well aware of the drama Jada's ex-husband put her through. In the midst of her darkest moments, Brenda had been a comforting shoulder for her to cry on.

"What's going on with him and his wife?" she wondered.

"I don't think she loves him," Jada said. "I mean, I know it's not my place to say that, but Evan feels that way too. You know how it is when a sick husband is in the hospital, and the wife is there every day... Everyone on the floor knows what a real marriage looks like, especially when the husband or wife is suffering."

Brenda nodded knowingly.

"What kind of wife goes days without visiting — doesn't bother coming to support him when he has a major procedure? Last night she came and argued with him, to the point where we had to go check on him because his heart rate spiked. Evan needs peace and love and understanding right now, and he's not getting it from her. I just want him to be happy."

"Do you think he can find happiness with you?"

Jada shrugged. "You know that can never work. He's my patient. Even if he wasn't married, we still can't be together. I don't know if there's a rule against it, but it's definitely frowned upon. Anyway, he *is* married, so that closes the door on us."

"If you never talked to him about your feelings, what made you fall in love?"

Jada's smile was soft and sweet as she considered that. "He's kind," she said. "He's so sweet. He's funny. Sometimes I'd go to his room, and we'd just talk, about his job and his life. I'd go home thinking about him all night. He's down to earth, and he's successful. He's strong, even with all that's going on with his heart."

Her friend smiled too. "Is he handsome?"

Jada's smile deepened. She nodded. "He's very good-looking."

"Hmmm. I don't know, Jada. If his wife is as bad as you say, and he feels the same way about you, maybe y'all could find a way to be together."

"You mean if he divorces her..."

"Yeah," Brenda said with a sigh. "I guess that's gotta come first. Are you willing to wait until he figures out what he's gonna do?"

"Yeah. It's not like I have a choice."

Her friend raised a skeptical eyebrow but didn't press her. Instead she asked, "Are you gonna eat that?" looking down at Jada's glazed salmon.

"Of course," she said, lifting her fork. "It's my favorite." She didn't have an appetite until the first tender morsel encountered her taste buds. After that, she was suddenly ravenous. "Ooh, girl, this is good! You wanna try some?"

On her second day off, Jada was overcome with a sense of foreboding when she received a call from her floor. She had told her friend they wouldn't call to notify her if Evan took a turn for the worst, but her mind wouldn't let go of the feeling that the call had something to do with him. Her fingers trembled slightly as she accepted the call.

"Hel, hello?"

"Hey, Jada." It was Sheila, the dayshift charge.

"Hi. Wha, what's going on?" *Jeez.* Jada couldn't believe her heart was beating so fast. *What in the world is going on with me?*

"We had a call-in," Sheila announced.

Jada brought a hand to her face and blew out a pent-up breath. *Oh, thank God.*

"I know you don't usually work the night shift," the charge nurse said, "but I'll buy you lunch, if you can do us a solid. I already called all the 7p nurses who are off. None of them can come. If you can't, I understand. They'll just have to work short."

"You mean today?"

"Yeah. I know it's not much notice..."

Jada checked the time. It was 3pm. If she agreed to do it, she could nap for a couple of hours before she had to get ready for work. But the 7p to 7a shift was a different kind of beast. The work got so slow in the wee hours of the morning, when all of the patients were asleep, staying awake would feel like torture. Jada had only worked the nightshift once in all the years she'd been a nurse. Even with seven hours sleep, that night had been one of her worst at the hospital.

"I'll do it," she said.

Sheila was surprised. "You sure? Did you get enough rest today? Did you sleep late?"

Jada actually woke up at seven that morning and had been running errands ever since, but she said, "Yeah, I slept late, and I have time to take a nap. I'll be alright."

She realized she had told another lie, a little white one, but it was still a lie. Once again, there was no need for it. This time, she knew why she was being deceitful.

Evan.

She was willing to say or do whatever was necessary to see him. Maybe she couldn't be honest with others, but she was past the point of lying to herself.

"Great!" Sheila said. "I owe you big time. Actually, night shift owes, you, 'cause I'm getting my tail out of here at seven. See you soon."

Jada wasn't able to sleep when she got off the phone. She knew she'd regret it later, but she couldn't stop her mind from racing. She lie in bed for the next two hours with her eyes shut, her thoughts on room 22.

She arrived on the unit at 6:30 that evening and took report from the day nurse. She was disappointed to learn

Evan was not one of the patients she was assigned to. On dayshift, Sheila would've made sure Jada kept the same patients, but the night charge simply assigned her to the open shift. Jada was not deterred from visiting with him at least once that night.

She waited until 7:30 before she approached Evan's nurse.

"Hey, Adam, 22 is my patient on dayshift. Is it okay if I pop in on him, to see how he's doing?"

He shrugged. "I don't care. Want me to ask Donna to swap him for one of your patients?"

Jada considered that for a moment before deciding against it. "No. All of our patients are on the same wing. You'd have to walk all the way across the unit to get to one of my patients."

"I don't mind."

Jada was tempted, but she had to be wary of the optics. If she used continuity of care as an excuse, the charge might want to know why she wasn't requesting *all* of her dayshift patients. "No, I don't want to switch," she told Adam. "I just want to check on him."

Evan's door was open, but she knocked before entering.

"Come in," she heard him call from inside.

Hearing his voice made her heart dance. When she entered the room, Jada was pleased to see his daughter seated next to his bed.

"Hey, how y'all doing?" Jada said.

Evan's eyes lit up. She knew he'd be surprised. His reaction was worth every bit of agony she might be experiencing by 4 a.m.

"Jada! What are you doing here?"

She laughed at him. "I work here, silly."

"But never on the night shift." He sat up to get a good look at her.

"Hi, Sharelle," Jada said to his daughter. "How's your summer going?"

"Good," Sharelle said. "Did Dad tell you I'm getting married?"

Jada's eyebrows raised.

"Not for at least a year," Evan interjected. "She's supposed to be bringing that boy to the hospital, so I can have a talk with him."

"*That boy*?" Sharelle said with a smirk. "He has a name, Dad."

"Yeah, and get this," Evan told Jada. "His name is *Earl*. What the hell kind of name is that?"

Jada couldn't help but laugh.

"What's wrong with Earl?" Sharelle said.

"Nothing," Jada replied. "It's a nice name. I'm just laughing at the way your father's acting. I'm not your nurse tonight," she told Evan, "but if you need anything, you can let me or Adam know. I just came to say hi. I might be back later. I gotta go check on my patients."

"Okay," Evan said. "It was good seeing you."

When she walked out, Sharelle said, "You really like her, don't you?"

"Yeah, I do," Evan told her. "We get along well. She's a good nurse."

"I like her too. I'm all for anything that keeps my daddy happy."

settled down by then. All of the patients were in their rooms, either getting ready for bed or already asleep. The nurses were scattered throughout the unit, some at their portable computers in the hallways, others chatting at the nurses' station. When she walked into his room, Jada found Evan sitting up watching TV. He greeted her with a warm smile.

"Hey."

"Hi," she said. "How you holding up?"

"I'm doing good," he said.

"Not hating it here anymore?"

He shook his head. "Nope. Not right now at least."

She pushed one of the chairs closer to his bed and took a seat. To her recollection, this was the first time she had ever sat down in his room. It was nice to interact with him at eye level. Evan thought so too.

"You're sitting down," he said. "Does this mean you can stay for a while?"

She smiled. "No, not necessarily. The thing about night shift is the staff doesn't have a lot to do when the patients are asleep, which means they're watching people even more, gossiping mostly."

He nodded. "You work night shift often?"

"No. I've only done it one other time."

"Do you like it?"

She shook her head.

"What made you decide to do it today?" he asked.

"They called and told me they were short. They needed someone to come in to help."

"Won't it throw off your sleep schedule?"

She nodded. "It'll take a day to get back on track. I'll take a nap when I get home, but I can't sleep too long, or else I won't be able to go back to sleep at nighttime."

"I don't think I'd be able to do it," Evan said. "I had a night job once when I was in college. I worked it for a week. I had to quit, because I kept falling asleep in class the next day."

"It is a sacrifice," Jada agreed. "But it comes with the job."

He sighed. Jada watched his chest rise and fall beneath his sheets. She knew his heart still had a lot of life left in it.

"I'm glad you're here," he told her. "When they told me you were off for the next four days..." He shook his head. "I couldn't hide my disappointment."

"I didn't want to be off for four days," Jada confided. "Not with you here."

He grinned at that. "Did you work tonight because of me?"

She grinned too. "Would it make you happy if I said yes?"

He nodded.

She switched gears. "What happened with you and your wife the other day?"

His smile was gone in an instant. "Same old, same old. Sometimes I can tolerate the way she treats me, the coldhearted things she says. But that night..." He frowned. "I don't think I can do it anymore. I know she's under a lot of stress, but I don't like being her punching bag. She was complaining about things at home that needed to be taken care of. She knows I'm in no position to help her right now. I don't know why she wants to make me feel inadequate. I feel bad enough as it is, being in the hospital all the time. I don't need to keep hearing how I'm failing her as a husband and as a man."

Jada's heart bled for him. "I don't think you're failing as a man. You're one of the strongest men I know."

"I can barely walk down the hall with a walker."

"I talked to your therapist. He said you were doing great. He didn't tell you how proud of you he was?"

"He did."

"Sometimes you have to take your victories in baby steps. Walking down the hallway is a big accomplishment, for someone who had heart surgery less than a week ago."

He cocked his head slightly. "Why do you like me so much, Jada?"

She chuckled. "Why do you ask me that?"

"I told you; all I've been hearing is how I'm not good enough. How useless I am."

"Your friends and family don't feel that way. I know your daughter tells you how awesome you are every time she sees you."

"But I don't hear it from my wife."

Jada understood what he wanted from her. She didn't think it was a good idea to substitute the affection he should be getting from his wife, but she understood why he needed it.

"I think you're smart," she said. "And funny. I love the relationship you have with your daughter. That's one of the qualities I admire the most about you. I grew up around a lot of girls who didn't have a father in their lives. I love to see a black man with a good relationship with his children, especially if it's a daughter."

Evan's smile broadened.

"I think you're strong," she said. "You have so many obstacles in your life, but you keep fighting. It's been eight years since you were first diagnosed. Since then, you've done all these procedures, taken all these meds, been hospitalized countless times. I know it seems like every time you take a step forward, something happens to push you two steps back. But you keep fighting.

"I've seen a lot of patients get depressed to the point where they want to give up. Once they give up mentally, the body starts to shut down. People don't believe it, but it's like I keep telling you; in order to heal, you have to be strong in the mind and the body. You have to believe you can get better, or you won't.

"I feel like I've gotten to know you very well, since I've been your nurse. A lot of nurses here think a good patient is one who doesn't give them any problems, doesn't ask for anything, doesn't keep pushing the call button. But you're my favorite patient because you're kind and considerate, and you're a fighter. Your energy makes my spirit stronger."

She watched his eyes, smiling. "Is that what you wanted to hear?"

He chuckled. "Yeah, it is. Thank you. I really needed that."

She checked the time.

Rather than complain about her leaving, he said, "Is this our last visit for the night?"

"I think so," she said, meeting his eyes again. "The later it gets, the harder it will be for me to explain why I'm in here."

"Have people started asking about us?"

She pursed her lips. "A little."

"What are they saying?"

"Just being nosey. They wanted to know why I visited you on the other floors."

"What'd you tell them?"

"I told them I've been your nurse for eight years, and there's nothing wrong with me wanting to check on you and see how you're doing."

"Am I getting you in trouble?" he wondered.

"Evan, don't worry about the gossips here. No one in this hospital is going to keep me from checking on you. If I have to see you on another floor or come in on my day off... Whatever it takes, I'll always be here for you."

Evan's heart fluttered. Surely she knew her words gave him life. His heart thudded as he considered his next question. He feared the life she had just given him could be taken away just as quickly.

"Jada, is it common for a patient to fall in love with his nurse?"

Her throat caught. He watched her eyes dilate. Her eyelids fluttered before she responded.

"Um, no, Evan. It's not common, but it does happen. When people are scared and vulnerable, they appreciate the people they believe are saving them. Sometimes that appreciation manifests as affection. It's called the Florence Nightingale effect."

"Why do they call it that?"

Her breaths came in shudders. "I don't, I don't know."

"Is it common for a nurse to fall in love with a patient?" he asked.

She shook her head. "No. That's not common."

"Has it ever happened to you? Have you ever fallen in love with a patient?"

She continued to shake her head as she rose from her seat. Her legs were unsteady. She prayed he wouldn't notice. "No, Evan. I haven't. I – I'm sorry."

She left the room without another word.

CHAPTER ELEVEN

TWO STEPS BACK

When Jada returned to work three days later, she was not happy with the report she received on her favorite patient.

"Dr. Davi wants to keep him a while longer."

"How much longer?"

"I don't know, at least a week."

Jada frowned. "Why? What happened?"

Evan's night shift nurse told her, "His rhythm changed to AFib the other day, and he's been going in and out of it ever since."

Jada's mouth went dry. Atrial fibrillation is an irregular, usually rapid heartbeat that occurs when the two upper chambers experience chaotic electrical signals. The rhythm wasn't uncommon for patients on the floor, but Jada knew it could lead to an increased chance of stroke and heart failure.

She was reminded of when she told Evan it might feel like every time he took a step forward, life seemed to push him two steps back. She wondered how he was taking the new diagnosis. She didn't have to wait long to find out.

"Ever since Dr. Davi talked to him," the nurse said, "he's been in a funk. He's not eating much, and he didn't want to do his physical therapy the other day. I think he's headed downhill."

It broke Jada's heart to hear that. "Has he been getting visitors?"

"His daughter's been here every night. But I think she's the only one. His wife hasn't been here since that incident earlier this week."

Jada sighed. "Okay. Thank you."

She stopped by Evan's room an hour later and found him asleep. Rest was probably the best thing for him. She quietly backed out of the room.

After lunch, his physical therapist came for their daily regimen. Jada watched him walk his patient out of the room on a walker. Evan looked to the nurses' station and spotted his favorite nurse. His features didn't light up like they usually did, but he nodded to her as a form of greeting. Jada forced a bright smile.

"Good afternoon, Evan!"

He gave her a brief smile, before his therapist led him in the opposite direction. Jada wanted to monitor his progress with the therapy, but a monitor tech pulled her attention away.

"24 just pushed the call button. She's complaining of chest pain."

Jada checked the monitors. The patient in C324 had a normal rhythm. "How long ago did she notify you?"

"A couple of minutes ago. She called earlier asking what her heart rate was. I gave it to her. This time she said she had chest pain. I think she just wants someone to talk to."

Jada agreed with his assessment. 24 was a widower, in her mid-eighties. She hadn't had any visitors in the week she'd been on the unit.

"Okay, I'll go talk to her."

She looked Evan's way again before heading to the other patient's room. He had his back to her, taking slow, shuffling steps down the hallway. His therapist followed close behind him, ready to catch him if he fell.

The patient in 24 wanted an update on her prognosis, a glass of water, a serving of apple sauce and then help getting to the bathroom. She talked Jada's ear off the whole time. Jada had suspected loneliness was the main reason she kept pressing the call button. She hated to see the elderly with no support system.

By the time she returned to the nurses' station, Evan was no longer walking around the unit. She headed for his room and saw his therapist exiting with the walker he had brought with him. Jada caught up with him before he made it to the elevators.

"Hey, Aaron, how's 22 doing?"

The therapist turned to face her. "I think he's just going through the motions," he said with a shake of his head. "When we first started, he was pretty gung ho. These last few days, he hasn't been giving a hundred percent."

"He's been in and out of AFib," Jada said. "Do you think that has something to do with it? Did Dr. Davi alter his therapy?"

Aaron shook his head. "No. Dr. Davi updated me on his condition, but she didn't change his regimen. The only thing she wants is for me to end the session for the day if he starts sweating and gets short of breath. But Shales isn't pushing himself hard enough to get out of breath. They'll probably call a code on him soon."

Jada's heart sank even deeper. The hospital called a Code Blue overhead when a patient's heart stopped beating. The alarm sent nurses and techs scrambling to the room. Any doctors in the vicinity had to head that way too. The casual way in which Aaron predicted the worst-case scenario for Evan made her nauseous. But she knew he hadn't spoken with malice or callousness. On any given day, three or four of the hospital's 800 patients coded. Most of the time, the staff could predict it beforehand.

"Thanks," she told Aaron.

She turned, intending to go to Evan's room, but when the elevator dinged behind her, a familiar face stepped out. It was Sharelle. Jada wasn't surprised that she looked a little worse for wear. When they made eye contact, Jada knew she had something on her mind. Sharelle waited until the therapist took the elevator she'd just vacated before she approached her father's nurse.

"Hi, Sharelle. How's everything going?"

The girl shook her head. "Not good. Have you talked to my dad today?"

"No. I've been meaning to, but I haven't had a chance yet. Why? What's up?"

"While you were gone, they said his heart started having AFib," Sharelle told her. "Ever since then, he's been acting depressed. He's not happy or joking like usual. I feel like he's giving up."

Jada didn't think she could feel worse about the things she'd been hearing that morning. But the distress in Sharelle's voice hit her soul even harder.

"I'll talk to him," she promised. "Go ahead and have your visit, and we'll see if he's feeling better afterwards."

Jada waited and kept an eye on Evan's room for the next few hours. A couple of times she thought Sharelle had left, and she had missed her. But when she casually walked by Evan's door, she heard him and his daughter speaking inside. Towards the end of the shift, Jada didn't think she'd have time for a one-on-one conversation with him, but she looked up from the nurses' station and saw Sharelle exit the room. The girl looked her way and saw Jada speaking with another nurse. She decided not to interrupt. She waved goodbye and headed for the elevator.

By the time Jada tore herself away from her coworker, Sharelle was no longer on the unit. That was just as well. It was better to gather the information she needed straight from the horse's mouth.

She walked into Evan's room without knocking. She found him lying on his back. His television wasn't on, and he didn't have his cellphone in hand. As far as she could tell, he was just lying there, staring at the ceiling. He looked her way briefly before his eyes rolled back to the ceiling. Jada frowned as she took a seat in the chair his daughter had been occupying.

She sat quietly for a few beats, watching him. He didn't say anything.

"*Hellooo*," she said. "You alright today?"

He sighed. "Did you hear about my new issue?"

"Yes. I talked to Dr. Davi."

"She told you she was keeping me longer, for observation?"

"Yes, she told me that. Is that what you're upset about?"

He shrugged. "I guess being here is just as bad as going home."

Her eyes narrowed. "Evan, what happened to that fighting spirit you had? You gonna let one little setback do you in?"

He turned to look at her. "You think *AFib* is a little setback?"

"I think half the patients on this floor have it. Some of the others have had it at some point. It's not a death sentence."

"With everything else I already got going on, it might be a death sentence for me."

She chuckled, hoping to lighten the mood. "Evan, you weren't feeling this bad when you had to have freaking *heart surgery*. How is this worse than that?"

"It's, I guess it's an accumulation of things. After a while, it gets to be too much."

"What happens when you feel like it *is* too much?" she wondered.

He shook his head. "I don't know."

She bit her bottom lip and gathered her thoughts before proceeding. "Evan, the way you're feeling now, does it have anything to do with the last thing we talked about?"

She thought he'd avoid the topic by looking away again, but he maintained eye contact. His stare was so deep, she felt like he could read her mind.

He didn't respond.

"Listen," she said. "When you asked me that, I gave you the only response I could give you."

He perked up. She could see that she'd lit a fire behind his eyes.

He asked, "What do you mean?"

"Evan, I'm your nurse. It's not right for a nurse to have a relationship with a patient. Besides that, you're married. That's why I didn't want to listen to anything negative you had to say about your wife. I don't think you've ever cheated before—"

"I haven't," he said, cutting her off.

"I didn't think you had. But I know a lot of people who have had affairs, most of them at this hospital, and I know that's how it starts. People wonder why most affairs start at the workplace. It's because we're with our coworkers for eight to twelve hours a day. We talk to them, laugh with them and eat with them for more time than we spend with our spouses.

"When we have a friend at work who's the opposite sex, and we start complaining about what our husband isn't doing and how we're so unhappy at home, it's easy for them to say how we don't deserve it, how smart and beautiful we are, how we'd be better off without them. Before you know it, you end up falling in love with someone who started off as your confidant. I've been working here for 24 years. Believe me, I know all the signs."

Evan nodded. "I understand. But just because that's how it usually happens doesn't mean it's the same for us. And if you gave me the response you felt like you had to give me, that doesn't mean you told me the truth."

Jada's face heated.

He asked her, "Do you want to know who Florence Nightingale was?"

She was surprised by the question, but she remembered telling him she didn't know the history behind the Florence Nightingale effect. At the time, Evan didn't know either.

She nodded. "You've done some research?"

"Yeah. She was an English nurse during the 1800s. During the Crimean war, she cared for wounded and dying soldiers. They called her 'the lady with the lamp,' because she would visit patients at night, carrying her lamp. Someone wrote a short poem about her. I saved it on my phone. I was gonna show it to you..."

"Do you still have it? I'd like to see it."

He found his phone on the bed and pressed a few buttons until he found the poem.

He started to hand the phone to her, but she said, "Do you want to read it?"

He watched her for a second before nodding.

"Okay. *Lo! in that house of misery, a lady with a lamp I see, pass through the glimmering gloom, and flit from room to room.*'" He shrugged. "It's not much."

"I like it," Jada said. "I think it's beautiful."

"I, uh. I like it too. It reminds me of you."

She smiled warmly.

"Before her, nurses didn't use to visit their patients at night," Evan told her. "I guess that's why some of the patients fell in love with her. Or maybe she was having relations with some of them, while everyone else was asleep."

Jada chuckled. "That sounds like something that would happen at this hospital."

Evan said, "I understand what you're saying about a patient being off limits, as far as a relationship. I also get why you think I might be confused about the way I feel about you. But none of that has changed my mind. I know it's wrong, especially since I'm married. The thing is, my heart has been hurting for a long time, Jada, physically and emotionally. My heart feels alive when I'm around you. I've felt like this for a long time, long before this current round of treatments. I'm sorry, but I don't want this feeling to go away."

He watched her for a long time. He could see the turmoil he'd caused her. He understood her conflict.

"Evan—"

"You don't have to say anything right now. I spoke my peace, and I feel better than I've felt all day." He checked the clock. "Your shift's about to end. Why don't you go home and think about what I told you, and you can give me a response in the morning."

She smiled. "Oh, now you're the one who thinks I've been in your room for too long?"

"One of us has to look out for your career," he joked. "Go home. Get some rest. I'll talk to you tomorrow."

"I, um, I'm off tomorrow, Evan."

His eyes widened. "What? You just got back."

"I only work three days a week. I usually like to have them in a row, but sometimes it doesn't work out that way."

"Three days a week? I don't think I've ever noticed that."

"You've never been on this unit for so long."

"Okay, well, I'll see you the day after tomorrow then?"

She nodded. "You okay with waiting?"

He shrugged. "Looks like I don't have a choice."

"Is it going to make you depressed?" she asked, "because I need you to take your physical therapy seriously."

He grinned sheepishly. "Aaron told you?"

"We're all in this together. I keep telling you; healing starts with the mind. The mind leads, and the body will follow."

"I'll do better," he said.

"Alright, Evan. I'll see you when I get back."

"Okay, Jada. Goodnight."

Jada's next day off wasn't as stressful as the last one, when she thought she wouldn't see Evan for four days. She knew that when she saw him again, he would want a response to the things he had told her. But she wasn't filled with a sense of foreboding.

When she returned to work, his nighttime nurse gave her an update that put a smile on her face.

"22's doing a lot better."

"Is he?"

"Yeah. He only converted to AFib once last night. And he's been a lot more talkative than the last couple of days. His therapist has seen a change in him too. Aaron says he's fighting now. He wants to get better. Everybody's wondering what lit a fire under his ass."

Jada was elated. She didn't think she'd said or done anything to change his disposition so drastically, but it was okay to take a little credit for turning him around.

When she went to check on him later, she found his tech Trisha changing the dressing on his chest wound. Jada hadn't seen his incision very often. She marveled at his toned upper body and his scar as she approached the bed.

"Morning," she told him.

He looked into her eyes. "Hey, Jada."

"How's it going in here?" she asked the tech.

Trisha was gently applying antibacterial ointment with a gloved hand. "*It's going,*" she said. "They been running me ragged since I got here. I can't even–"

Another nurse stepped into the room, interrupting her. "Oh, there you are, Trisha. I was looking for you. When you get done in here, one of my patients needs to be cleaned. I keep telling Dr. Mitchell that man needs to be in a diaper, but nope. She thinks it's okay if he keeps pooping on himself."

She walked away without waiting for a response.

"See what I mean," Trisha said with a frown.

Evan laughed.

"Yeah, you got a lot going on," Jada noticed.

"Tell me something," Trisha said to her. "How come when y'all nurses get your degree, you forget what it's like to be a PCT? Most of y'all worked as techs while you were in school. You know what it was like to work under nurses who made you do all the dirty work. But when y'all become nurses, you turn around and do the same thing to *your* techs."

"I hope I'm not like that," Jada said. "I try to help out as much as possible. As a matter of fact, I don't mind finishing up in here."

"Why you didn't offer to let *me* finish up in here and *you* take care of that mess down the hall?" Trisha asked sarcastically.

"Oh, hell no!" Jada said. "I went to school so I wouldn't have to wipe asses no more," she joked.

"That's exactly what the hell I'm talking about!" Trisha couldn't help but laugh as she backed away from the bed and removed her gloves. "I appreciate you finishing up with this one," she said as she left the room. "You ain't like those other nurses."

Jada washed her hands at the sink in the room and pulled on a pair of gloves before approaching Evan's bed. Trisha was mostly done with the ointment, but Jada didn't think it would hurt to apply a little more – and it definitely wasn't because she relished the opportunity to touch his smooth, dark chest. She could tell Evan appreciated their closeness as much as she did.

"My daughter says it looks like I got a zipper going down my chest," he told her.

The wound ran from between his clavicles down past his pectorals. Until the staples were removed, Jada thought Sharelle's comparison was spot on.

"It's healing well," she replied. "It'll be barely noticeable in a couple of months."

"My uncle had heart surgery. It's been years, and I can still see his scar every time we go to the beach."

"This scar gives you character," she said, her eyes on her work.

"Always the optimist."

She nodded. "You like that about me."

He grinned. "I do." Then, "Have you given any thought to what we talked about?"

She knew that would be one of the first things he'd ask her. She had plenty of time to come up with a response, but she couldn't give him anything definite.

"I've thought about it," she said. "It's all I've been thinking about."

"And..."

She looked up at him and nearly got lost in his dark eyes. Her expression became serious, almost pained. "Evan, I keep thinking that – if only you weren't married. I think I'd be okay with dealing with the problems I'd have at work, but the marriage... You know my husband cheated on me. I know how that betrayal feels. Even if your wife treats you horribly, you're still married to her. I can't be the other woman. I just–"

He reached up unexpectedly. She didn't know what to expect until his hand slipped into her frizzy mane. His fingers slid smoothly to the back of her head and urged her forward.

Jada's heart froze. The blinding shift of energy in the room overpowered the million thoughts raging through her brain – the most urgent of which being the fact that the door to his room was open, and though it had been a while since this had happened to her, she knew Evan wanted to kiss her.

Oh, God.

As their lips inched closer, she realized his hand behind her head was unnecessary. His head had barely risen from his pillow, yet the distance between them steadily decreased. And though his hand was unnecessary, it felt so good to have him touch her like that. The feel of his bare chest felt good too. Jada didn't realize her palm was flat on his pectoral. She rubbed him tenderly, needing to feel his heat and his energy, the steady beat of his heart.

When their lips touched, the blistering wave of uncertainty collided with the fear of the taboo, and though she knew the door was wide open behind her, she couldn't stop herself from moaning slightly as she sucked his lips and he sucked hers. Her blood became a tsunami, rushing through her veins at dangerous speeds.

Rationale kicked in just as quickly, and she forced herself to withdraw.

Her eyes were wide, her breaths heated. Evan's expression seemed calm by comparison. He watched her closely, his eyes steely, his lips still slightly puckered. Oh how handsome he was! Jada didn't know how that just happened, but her complete being begged for it to happen again. She looked back to make sure no one was coming.

What in the fuck–

How could she seriously be considering that??

"Evan," she breathed. "We can't"

He released her immediately. She realized she could've stopped this travesty before it started, if she'd uttered those words sooner.

"I got, I gotta..." She reached blindly, unwilling to tear her eyes away from his. Her hand finally encountered the gauze and bandage Trisha had left. "I gotta wrap you," she told him.

He nodded and sat up, so she could wrap the bandage fully around his torso. This was what she expected him to do, but the sudden movement made her think he was leaning in for another kiss. She wasn't completely relieved when she realized he wasn't.

Her trembling fingers matched the rest of her quivering body as she wrapped him quietly and carefully. Neither of them spoke another word. Jada didn't breathe a sigh of relief until she left the room and saw that no one was standing outside the door, and none of the staff was aware of what had happened.

CHAPTER TWELVE
WET

Over the next couple of days, Evan continued to show strides in his recovery. Jada ran into his cardiologist one morning, while Dr. Davi was visiting other patients on the unit. She approached her in the hallway.

"How are you, doctor?"

"I'm fine, Jada. How are you?"

"I'm good. I hear Shales is doing a lot better."

"Yes, he's reaching the criteria for discharge. He should be headed home soon."

"What criteria are you looking for with him?"

"Well, he's having bowel movements."

Jada grinned. "Yes, I believe he's okay with that."

"Is he able to get out of bed for meals?"

"His therapist left him a walker. He has to use it sometimes."

"That's alright," the doctor said. "He tells me his pain level is minimal, and it's manageable with meds."

Jada nodded.

"As long as he's able to eat and drink, and he can walk, either with the walker or without, then there's only one thing left."

Jada was surprised by how she was hoping for something Evan hadn't accomplished yet. For the life of her, she didn't believe she'd ever felt that way about a patient.

"What's the last thing?" she asked.

"I'm waiting for his vital signs to stabilize. I'm willing to discharge him with the AFib, but he's had episodes of AFib with RVR. I won't feel comfortable sending him home while that's happening."

Jada knew having a rapid ventricular rate could be dangerous. To her recollection, Evan only had that rhythm twice since he started having AFib.

"I'm giving him meds for that," his cardiologist stated. "If he doesn't have any more occurrences in the next few days, I'll be ready to discharge him."

"That's great," Jada said. "Have you told him yet?"

The doctor shook her head. "No. You can give him the good news, if you like."

Jada visited with her favorite patient during lunchtime. Evan was seated on the side of the bed with his bed table positioned over his lap. She watched him for a few seconds, noticing he was comfortable, maintaining the seated position with no signs of pain or discomfort, and he had a hearty appetite. None of the other patients on the floor were that engrossed with their tuna sandwiches.

"Hungry today?" she asked.

He nodded. "Yeah, I guess so. My mom used to make tuna sandwiches for lunch, when we were out of school for the summer. I haven't had very many since I was little. This sandwich brought back a lot of memories."

"I'm glad you're enjoying it. I spoke to Dr. Davi this morning."

"What'd she say?" he asked around his sandwich.

"She's getting close to discharging you."

Evan stopped eating in midbite. He appeared to have to force the last mouthful down his throat. "When?" he asked.

"She's waiting for your heart rhythm to stabilize."

"She wants to keep me until I don't have AFib?"

"No, it's the RVR she's worried about. I know it only happened a couple of times. She says if you don't have anymore episodes in the next few days, she'll feel comfortable sending you home."

He replied with a subdued, "Hmmm."

"*Hmmm*? I don't think I've ever gotten that reaction from a patient, when it came to them going home. Do you like the food here that much?" she kidded.

He offered her a half smile. "You know that's not it."

"What is it then?"

"This is the only place I get to see you."

She nodded. "I know, Evan."

"You're okay with that?"

"I don't, I'm not sure how to feel about it. Earlier today I found myself rooting for you to have more RVR, and I know that's not right."

"It wouldn't be the worst thing."

"Evan, that's a dangerous heart rhythm. I should never wish anything like that on a patient."

"What if I get sick again when I get home?"

"I don't think you will, but if you have to come back, we'll be ready to get you healthy again."

He sighed.

"Evan, please don't be like that. Getting out of the hospital is a good thing. It's what we've all been working for. All of the staff at this hospital has the same goal. But you should want this more than any of us. I understand your worries about your heart... and about us. Everything will be fine. Trust me."

He looked into her eyes and nodded.

"Now are you gonna finish that sandwich, or do I have to tell Dr. Davi you're not eating well?"

"Will that keep me in the hospital longer?"

"Boy, if you don't finish that sandwich...!" she snapped.

Evan laughed and took another big bite. "Yes, ma'am."

Later in the shift, the floor's monitor tech alerted Jada to a rising heart rate in C322.

"Hey, Jada. Check this out."

She looked over his shoulder and saw that Evan had spiked up to the 100's.

"How long has it been like this?"

"It just happened," he said.

As they watched, his leads began to flatline, one at a time.

Jada's eyes widened as the asystole alarm went off. It was a blaring alarm that overrode all of the others.

Jada jumped into action. Her PCT was right behind her.

Jada's heart rattled in her throat as they rushed into the room. They found Evan's bed empty. The portable monitor mounted on his IV pole displayed the same reading they'd seen at the nurses' station. The IV pole was next to the bathroom door, rather than on the side of his bed where it usually was. As she moved closer, Jada saw that the electrodes dangling from the monitor box were on the floor, rather than connected to the patient.

A wave of relief rushed over her. The electrodes weren't sophisticated enough to know when there was no heart activity or when they'd been removed from the patient. The monitor simply recognized there was no heart rhythm, and it had done its job. Jada turned the monitor off to silence the alarm. When the room was quiet, she knocked on the closed bathroom door.

"Evan?"

From inside, she heard him say, "Yeah, I'm in here."

She asked him, "Did you take your leads off?"

"Yeah. I was gonna take a shower. I heard it going off. Did I mess something up?"

Jada's pulse was still recovering from the shock he'd given her. "No, it's alright. Do you still have your gown on? Do you need help?"

"Yeah, I have my gown on. I might need help getting some of these sticky pads off."

Jada pushed the door open and found him standing in the center of the bathroom, bracing himself with his walker. He wasn't sweating and didn't appear to be in distress.

"Have you been showering by yourself?" she asked him.

"No. Trisha's been helping me."

"He usually tells me when he's ready," Trisha chipped in.

Jada had almost forgotten the tech was standing at her side. "You're ready to try to shower by yourself?" she asked Evan.

"If I'm gonna be going home soon, I think it's time to see if I can do it," he replied. "I might not have any help when I get home."

Jada knew what he was alluding to. She was surprised by the jealousy that ensued. The thought of his wife helping him bathe didn't sit right with her.

"Alright, I'll help get the pads off, and we'll see if you're ready," she said as she stepped closer to him.

"Want me to do it?" Trisha asked.

"No, that's alright," Jada said. "It's no big deal."

Trisha left the restroom, and Jada closed the door behind her.

"You gave me quite a scare," she told her patient.

"I didn't mean to. I heard the alarm going off. I thought it would stop when I got all the leads off."

She shook her head. "It doesn't work like that. If you want to take your monitor off, you need to let us know ahead of time. Otherwise the machine will tell us you're not breathing."

"Oh. I guess that makes sense."

"You wanna take your gown off and get in the shower chair?"

His mouth fell open. "Oh, um... Right now?"

She grinned at him. "Evan, I'm your nurse. You said Trisha's been helping you shower. What's the difference now?"

"Well, um, I don't like her, not like that."

"You're embarrassed to be nude in front of your nurse?"

"No. I'm embarrassed to be nude in front of a woman I'm falling in love with."

Her face heated. "That's understandable. But right now you need to see me as your nurse, and we'll deal with the other part later. Now come on, let's get that gown off. Do you need help?"

He shook his head. "No. I'm supposed to be trying this on my own, right?"

She nodded.

He had to release the walker one hand at a time to get the gown off and maintain his balance, but he managed. The garment fell to the floor around his feet. Jada reminded herself to maintain objectivity when she saw his bare ass for the first time. He looked back at her.

"Like what you see?" he asked with a smirk.

"Please don't ask me that right now," she said with a chuckle. "Go ahead and get in your shower chair."

He walked the walker into the shower and half turned, until his backside was facing the chair. He took a seat and turned to look at her.

"Should I keep the walker in here with me?"

"How does Trisha usually do it?"

"She takes it out and helps me to it when we're done. But I think I should keep it in here, in case I have trouble getting up when I'm finished."

"Good idea."

She stepped into the shower with him and removed the electrode sticky pads from his torso. She didn't stare between his legs, but she couldn't help but notice his flaccid manhood. Even in an unaroused state, the sight of it made her chest shudder.

When she backed out of the shower, Evan turned on the water and proceeded to bathe himself. Jada half turned and watched her own reflection in the mirror. Neither of them spoke.

After a minute she asked him, "Do you want me to step out, until you're done?"

"You can," he said, "but Trisha has been helping wash my back. I have one of those back scrubbers in my shower at home."

"I could wash your back for you," she said, turning back to him.

As she stepped closer, she tried not to get lost in his smooth, dark skin. The shower nozzle was posited to spray just under his chin. The bathroom was already starting to get steamy.

When she was closer, he handed her the soap and wash cloth he was using. He leaned forward, lifting his back from the chair. Jada leaned over him and began to wash his back. Since becoming a nurse, she didn't bathe patients very often. She wondered how she used to avoid getting wet when she did it as a tech. Within a few seconds, she knew she'd have to find another scrub top when she was done. She might have to find a pair of scrub pants too.

Her focus was not between his legs as she washed him, but it was hard not to notice the change down there.

"Evan, what is happening?" she asked him.

He cleared his throat. "Um, what do you mean?"

"You know what I mean, sir."

He chuckled nervously. "I'm sorry. I didn't mean to."

"Does this happen when Trisha bathes you?"

He shook his head. "No. It never has. I told you I might have a problem if you were in here with me."

"You didn't say you'd have *that* kind of problem."

He looked up at her and was relieved that she was smiling, rather than offended.

"I didn't expect this kind of problem," he said. "This is embarrassing."

His manhood steadily grew. Jada didn't try to hide the fact that she was watching it now. It grew up past his belly button and kept growing. And then it began to pulsate.

"Jeez, Evan. What are you gonna do with that?"

"Nothing. It'll go away once I get back in bed. Could you, could we please stop talking about it. This is uncomfortable."

"This conversation is uncomfortable or your little problem is?"

He smirked at her. "You think it's little?"

She blushed. "Okay, we can stop talking about it."

"I haven't had sex in six months," he told her.

Her eyes widened. "I, uh, I don't think I needed to know that."

"I'm just letting you know, so you won't think I'm some kind of pervert."

"I don't think that."

"And your hands feel good on my back," he said. "With all this water, and you, the way you smell, your beautiful face... I don't think I could ever be naked around you, without this happening."

Jada knew there was no way to reestablish objectivity at that point. As fine as this man was, she couldn't help but be moved by his comment. Her ex-husband had scorned her, seeking sexual gratification in the arms of other women. Evan couldn't fight his desire for her, even in such an obscure setting.

Her thoughts swam as her right hand moved from his back to his front. She didn't try to fight the dizziness. She didn't want to think clearly about what was happening. If she hesitated, she would stop, and she didn't want to stop. When she wrapped her hand around his manhood, she knew Evan didn't want her to stop either. He leaned back against the chair. His chest swelled. His eyes slipped closed.

She felt the blood rushing through his swollen veins as she squeezed him, caressed him. She watched the ecstasy roll down his frame, starting in his face, rumbling through his chest, and peaking when it reached his erection.

He kept his arms by his sides. Other than the steady rise and fall of his torso, he didn't move at all while she stroked him. A cool burn in her chest descended past her belly and settled on her clit. The moistness in her panties matched the wetness in her hand, on her scrubs. She felt as if the whole room had become a warm, soothing waterfall.

Evan's body shuddered. His head rolled back, and his mouth fell open and a series of quiet moans preceded his eruption. She had only been stroking him for a little over a minute, giving credence to the timeframe he'd given her, since the last time he made love.

Jada couldn't take her eyes off his essence as it spewed from him. She was mesmerized by it. For now, at least, she did not feel shame for what she had done. She continued holding him, stroking slowly, until he was completely spent, and most of his cum had washed away.

Finally, she released him and repeated the question she'd asked a few minutes ago.

"Do you want me to step outside the bathroom, until you finish?"

This time he looked her in the eyes and said, "Um, yeah. I, um…" He swallowed. "I think that's probably for the best."

She helped Evan get his leads back on when he got back into bed. Things were a little awkward, but she performed her nurse duties as usual. They did not speak about what had transpired in the shower.

When she got back to the nurses' station, Jada asked the charge if they had a pair of scrubs she could change into.

"We have some surgical scrubs in the supply room," Sheila told her. She looked her up and down. "What happened?"

"I was helping 22 with a shower."

"I don't know how Trisha manages to stay so dry when she does that," the charge said.

"That's what I was wondering while I was in there," Jada replied with a laugh.

In the supply room, she frowned at the scrubs that were available for her. Her normal scrub suits weren't form fitting, but they weren't atrociously baggy like the surgical scrubs. She looked down at her outfit. She wasn't *soaking* wet. She wondered how long it would take for her to dry on her own if she carried on with her day.

Someone entered the room behind her. She looked back and greeted them.

"Hey, Trisha."

When the tech didn't respond, Jada turned to face her. She frowned at the look on Trisha's face.

"What's wrong?"

The tech stepped closer. Though the room was small, and the door was closed, she spoke with a hushed voice.

"Now, I'ma ask you again; what's going on with you and 22?"

Jada's heart froze. Even if she wanted to deny it again, her expression would've given her away.

Trisha's mouth fell open. *"Really, Jada?"*

"Shhh!" she told her.

"Don't *shhh* me," Trisha hissed. "Girl, what is wrong with you?"

"I don't know," Jada cried, her features crumbling. "I didn't want for any of this to happen. How, how did you know?"

"I know chemistry," Trisha said. "I told you I saw something in his eyes the first time I saw y'all together. And you offering to help him with his shower..."

"I offer to help you with patients all the time."

"Yeah, but it's different with that man, and you know it. Are y'all having a full-blown affair or just flirting?"

"I don't know," Jada said. "I feel horrible about the whole thing. Does anyone else know?"

"Well, I told you some nurses on C1 and C2 were asking questions. But no one thinks too much about it – *yet*. They will, if you keep going like you going."

"I'm not," Jada said. "I won't."

"You such a good nurse," Trisha said. "I'd hate for anything to happen to your career over something like this."

Jada shook her head. She was near tears.

"I love you, girl," Trisha said.

She reached to console her. Jada allowed herself to be wrapped up in a hug.

"If y'all are gonna continue this," Trisha said, "you need to wait till that man is out of the hospital – *and* not married."

"I know," Jada said, crying now. "I know I messed up. I'm sorry."

"You don't need to apologize to me," Trisha said, holding her tightly. "I'm just looking out for you and your job."

CHAPTER THIRTEEN

AN HONEST WOMAN

The next morning, Dr. Davi stopped by room C322 as she made her morning rounds. She found her patient sitting up in bed eating breakfast.

"Good morning, Evan."

"Morning, doc."

"How are you feeling today?"

"I feel good," he replied.

"How are you sleeping? Do you find yourself waking up at night with pain, sweating?"

"No. Sometimes when I roll over my chest hurts. I'm used to sleeping on my side, but I'm learning to sleep on my back."

"Good," she said. "I spoke with your monitor tech. He hasn't seen anymore instances of AFib with RVR."

Evan nodded. "Do I still have the AFib?"

"You only converted to AFib once yesterday. It lasted about five minutes. Your nurse says you don't feel any different when you convert."

Evan remembered having that conversation with Jada. "No, I don't feel anything."

"Perfect. That's what I wanted to hear. I know you've been anxious to go home. I'd like to keep you one more day, to make sure the RVR doesn't come back."

Evan brought a hand to his head and rubbed the side of his face.

"What's wrong?" Dr. Davi asked.

"I, uh…" He sighed. "I guess I'm scared, doc."

"What are you afraid of, Evan?"

"This last time I got admitted, it was because I had a heart attack. I remember lying in the grass in front of my house. I couldn't yell loud enough for my wife to hear me. As I felt myself passing out, I thought that was it. I didn't think I was gonna make it."

"I know, Evan. I understand that was a frightening experience."

"When I get home," he said, "I'm worried something else will go wrong. I don't wanna be in the hospital. Don't get me wrong. But at least I know I'm safe here. There's someone watching my heart rate all day long. I took my monitor off yesterday, and two people ran to my room within a minute."

The cardiologist smiled compassionately. "What you're experiencing is not uncommon, especially for heart patients. We all fear the unknown, Evan. You have to rely on your faith in God, your faith in your immune system and your faith in the treatment we've provided you. I pray for you, every night. I pray for all of my patients. I have faith that you will get better, despite all that has happened recently. I've always believed that."

Evan smiled too. Everyone he expressed his fears to had a similar response. If so many people believed in him, the least he could do was have faith in himself.

"Thanks, doc. That makes me feel a lot better."

Jada visited after lunch to make sure he was still eating well. Evan had just finished the hospital's infamous *mystery pasta*. Jada cringed when she saw that his plate had been scraped clean.

"Ooh. I'm glad you ate well, but I meant to give you a heads up before you got lunch, to see if you'd want me to get you a sandwich instead."

"Hmm?" He looked down at his plate. "What was wrong with my pasta?"

"What kind of pasta was it?"

He frowned and shrugged. "Umm... I don't know."

"Exactly," she said with a chuckle. "I see some toilet time in your future."

He laughed. "Okay. Thanks for the heads up. Hey, I talked to Dr. Davi this morning."

"What'd she say?"

"She's sending me home tomorrow, unless I have more RVR or anything else weird between now and then."

"That's great news, Evan."

"Yeah. I was nervous about it, but after talking to her, I feel better."

"I'm glad to hear that."

He watched her for a few seconds before saying, "I was wondering if I could get your number. I don't want to lose contact with you when I leave."

Considering how close they'd gotten, both emotionally and physically, it felt odd to be hesitant about exchanging numbers. But she couldn't deny her apprehension.

She told him, "I'll give it to you, but I don't like the idea of you calling me while you're at home with your wife. I told you; I don't want to be the other woman. After what my husband did to me, that's not a role I can play."

"I know how you feel. I don't want that for you either. I'm not trying to put you in an uncomfortable situation."

"I'm afraid you already have. But it wasn't just you. I did this to myself. I knew you were married. I never should've..."

"Please don't say that. I don't feel like what happened with us was a mistake. I don't want you to feel that way either."

She sighed. "I can't help it, Evan. We both know right from wrong. You know how I feel about this; even if your wife isn't treating you right, you're still married to her. I think..." She wiped her nose with the back of her hand, fighting back tears. "I think we should take a break."

His eyes registered immediate distress. "What kind of break? What do you mean?"

"I think we need to slow down, until you figure out what's going on with your wife. I want you to be happy, Evan. No matter what you decide."

"I'm happy with you."

"But you're with her."

He sighed. "You, you said you'd give me your number? Did you change your mind?"

She shook her head. "No. I'll give it to you. I wanna know how things are going when you leave here, as far as your health. But for now, I don't think we should take it past that."

She knew she was breaking his heart. The pain in his expression crushed her as well.

"Okay," he said, desperate to hold onto any communication she was offering. He lifted his phone from the bed and opened a new contact. He offered it to her.

Against better judgement, she took the phone and inputted her number.

A few hours later, Jada was surprised to see Delores on the unit. Evan's wife hadn't paid him a visit in over a week. From the nurses' station, Jada didn't get a good look at her, but she could tell Delores wasn't in good spirits.

Thirty minutes later, Evan's wife looked even more upset when she marched out of the room, her teeth clenched, her features set in a scowl. Jada was in the hallway at the time, three rooms down. The two women locked eyes, and Delores' sneer deepened. She growled, literally, loudly enough for another nurse in the hallway to hear her. Jada was stunned. She knew Delores remembered their last altercation, but it was shocking to see a woman growl at her. Her heart froze as the barracuda stormed past.

"What's wrong with her?" the other nurse in the hallway asked.

Jada shook her head. Her mouth was dry, her heart knocking. "I don't know."

"She's pissed."

Jada would've given him the Captain Obvious award if she wasn't so freaked out. She stepped away from her portable computer and went directly to Evan's room. He was seated on the side of his bed, his head down, his expression unreadable.

He looked up at her and said, "*Whew*. I guess you saw that."

"Yeah, I did," Jada replied, her breathing not yet under control. "What happened? What's wrong with her?"

He sighed and shrugged. "I told her."

Jada didn't think she could take much more stress. She placed a hand on the wall to brace herself. "Told her *what*?"

"I told her I'm not coming home tomorrow when I get discharged."

Jada was floored. Her eyes grew as big as quarters. "*You told her about us*?" she whispered.

"No, you, do you need to sit down?"

She did, but there was no way she'd get caught sitting in his room, especially not after what had just transpired between him and his wife.

"No. I'm, I'm alright."

"I told her I wanted a divorce, but I didn't say anything about you," Evan assured her.

Jada couldn't get her mouth to close.

"*Wha, why did you do that*?"

"What do you mean? I told you I wasn't happy with her. We talked about this. Why are you confused?"

"You didn't tell me you were going to ask for a divorce."

"I didn't know I was until after lunch. When I made up my mind, I called her and told her to come to the hospital. I told her it was very important. I'm surprised she came so quick."

Jada thought she might vomit. "Evan, I don't like the idea of you doing this – not for me."

"It's not all about you. We've had problems for years."

"But you didn't make this decision until after we talked. I don't' want to be the cause of your marriage ending."

"You're not the cause of it, Jada. This was already in the making."

"But you didn't do it until *after we talked*," she stressed.

"Okay," he conceded. "You gave me the courage to do something I should've done long ago. She's always put her career first. I tolerated it, but I couldn't pretend I was happy about it anymore – not after I got sick. I needed her, and she's been so cold to me, I felt like she would be the one who ended up killing me. I can't take any more of the stress she's causing me. You don't like being the catalyst. I get it. But damn. It seems like no matter what step I take, you're not happy with it."

Jada realized he was right. That didn't make the sick feeling go away.

"It's never been in me to be a cheater," he said. "And I know it's not in you either. I messed up. *We* messed up. I'm doing my best to make it right – for the both of us. I wanna make an honest woman of you. What I did today is hard for me, and I can see it's hard for you. But if we're gonna have a future together, this had to come first. I'm sorry, for everything – except leaving my wife. No matter what happens next, I'll never regret that."

A part of her felt this was the best possible outcome. But it didn't feel like it. Jada didn't think she'd ever felt so crummy and conflicted.

"I'm sorry," she said. "I don't mean to give you a hard time. I'm just, this is scary."

"I'm leaving the hospital with a bad heart, no home to go home to and a fresh separation from my wife. I got a lot more to be scared about."

Her eyes filled with tears. "I know you do, Evan. I'm sorry. We, we'll figure this out."

Jada wasn't aware that Evan's daughter had stopped by an hour later. When she went to see how he was doing and heard her voice inside, she returned to the nurses' station.

Inside his room, Evan had a third emotional breakdown on his hands. It was hard to maintain composure in the midst of his daughter's tears – tears he knew his selfishness caused – but if he was going to do something so monumental, he had to be man enough to look his loved ones in the eyes and take responsibility.

"Baby girl, I know this hurts you. It hurts me too."

"*Then why are you doing it?*" she bawled.

"I'm doing it for my peace of mind. "I'm doing it for my stress level, for my heart, for my life to feel normal again."

"Can't y'all work it out? You and mom hardly ever argue."

"No, we never argue *around you*. That's what good parents are supposed to do. If you think our marriage has always been perfect, that means we did a good job. But you don't know what it's been like for me. I love the fact that your mom's such a hard worker, but I need her to be there for me too. I've always needed her. I put my needs aside for years, but I couldn't do it anymore when my heart started failing me."

"Are you saying she won't take care of you?"

"No, I think she would. But it wouldn't be with a loving heart."

"How do you know that?"

"Because it's happening right now. If I told you some of the things she's said to me in the past few years..."

"Tell me. Tell me, Dad. What did she say that was so bad?"

He shook his head. "I know you're an adult, but I feel like I've already told you too much. At the end of this, she's still your mom, and I want you to love her today just as much as you did yesterday. I'm not gonna turn this into a situation where you have to pick a side. I don't want your mom to do that either, but I can't control what she does.

"I'm sorry you're upset. Seeing you like this hurts me more than anything. If it wasn't for you, our marriage never would've made it this far."

Seeing the tears in his eyes finally weakened Sharelle's resolve.

"I'm sorry, Daddy. I know this is hard for you too. I just wish it didn't have to happen. I never dreamed my parents would get a divorce. Out of all my friends, I'm the only one left whose parents are still together. I thought you and mom would love each other forever."

The tears streaming down her face were like daggers, each one piercing Evan's already wounded heart. Thank God this was the last of the people he had to hurt. No one else in his life would take the news this badly. Most of them would actually be supportive.

"Come here," he said softly.

Sharelle rose from her seat and stepped into his open arms. He wrapped her up in the biggest daddy hug he could muster and let her cry on his shoulder until her tears finally subsided.

Jada had been waiting on pins and needles since she realized Sharelle was in her father's room. It was shift change when the girl finally left. Jada struggled to maintain focus as she gave report to the nurse who was taking over her patients.

When she was done, she told her, "22 asked me something earlier, but I forgot what it was. Let me check to see what he wanted before I leave."

Her nerves were nearly shot when she slipped into his room. She found Evan lying in bed, looking through his phone. He turned her way and sighed.

"Oh, thank God."

She walked to his bed and placed her hands on the bedrail. "What do you mean?"

"I thought Delores was back with more drama."

Jada looked over her shoulder. "Are you expecting her to come back?"

"No. I'm just a little shell-shocked. I've had three horrible conversations with three women in the last seven hours. I don't think I can take any more of that today."

Jada nodded. "You should get some rest. Please try not to stress." Then, "You told your daughter?"

"Yeah," he said with a sigh.

"Did she, how did she take it?"

"As well as to be expected. She's devastated. But I think she understands why I had to do this."

Jada brought a hand to her mouth and nibbled on her thumbnail, a habit she hadn't entertained in years.

"You haven't changed your mind?" she asked.

He shook his head. "No. That's not gonna happen. I told you that was the one thing I'll never regret, no matter how the rest of this turns out."

She took a deep breath and exhaled slowly. "Okay. I, um, I gotta head home. Night shift is already here. They'll wonder why I'm in here, if I stay too long."

"I understand."

She wanted to hug him so badly, her heart cried.

"You really are the strongest man I know," she told him. "I don't like being in the middle of this, but what you're doing, at a time like this... It takes so much courage."

"I don't feel courageous. The only thing I feel right now is foolish for letting my marriage go on for so long. Will you be here tomorrow, when I get discharged."

"Yes, I'm working tomorrow."

"Okay, I guess I'll see you in the morning."

"Okay, Evan. Please get some sleep. I lov–" She caught herself. "I'll be thinking about you."

"You're all I'll be thinking about." He stared into her eyes so hard, her legs went weak. She turned and left the room, while she still had the strength to do so.

CHAPTER FOURTEEN
BARACUDA

The next afternoon, Evan was ready to be discharged from the hospital. He was surprised by how many belongings he'd accumulated since he'd been there. Aside from clothing and personal effects, he had an assortment of get-well cards and vases, some of which still had fresh flowers in them. He asked Jada if she could find somewhere to donate them in the hospital.

"I don't know if the gift shop will want the vases back," she said. "You're not infectious, but they're wary about taking things that came from a patient's room."

"I don't want to throw them away," Evan said, looking at the beautiful vases he'd lined up on his windowsill.

"Are you sure you don't want to take them with you?" Jada asked.

"Even if I was going home, I probably wouldn't. I try to keep the clutter at my house down to a minimum. But since I'm not going home, I definitely don't have anywhere to put them."

"Okay," Jada said. "I'll find something to do with them. If worse comes to worse, I can always recycle them."

"I guess that's better than the trash."

Jada nodded. They were quiet for a few moments.

"Are you ready for your discharge orders? I'm going to give you the paperwork, but I have to give some of them verbally."

"Yeah, I'm ready."

He sat on the side of the bed fully clothed in jeans, a tee shirt and sneakers. It was rare for Jada to see him in anything but a hospital gown. His outfit wasn't flashy, but she thought it was fashionable. Evan had said he was overdue for a haircut, but Jada thought he was as handsome as ever.

"Make sure you walk for at least thirty minutes, three times a day," she said. "No twisting, bending or strenuous activity for the next ten weeks. Try not to lift any item over five pounds. That's about the weight of a gallon of milk."

She looked down at the bags he'd packed.

"Will you have someone to help you with these?"

"Yeah. Sharelle's gonna help me get settled. She's on her way now."

"Okay. No sitting or standing for too long," Jada continued. "Make sure you get up and move around every two hours. Dr. Davi wants you to eat five to six small meals a day, instead of three big ones. You need to continue to shower instead of taking baths until your incision wound fully heals. And I have a list of your new meds. They've already been sent to your pharmacy. Will you have someone to take you to pick them up? You aren't supposed to drive while taking the pain meds."

"Yes, I'll have someone who can help me."

She looked over the rest of his orders. "I guess that's it. Everything else you need to know is here."

She handed him the papers. He took them and put them in the outer compartment of one of his bags. They watched each other.

When she didn't speak, he said, "You're starting to look like I did when I first found out I was getting discharged."

She sighed. "I'm sorry, Evan. I don't mean to sound like I'm down. I'm happy you're getting out of here. It's just…"

He waited and then asked, "Just what?"

"I can't say I'm happy about you going to a hotel."

He shook his head. "I'm not that thrilled about it either. But this is temporary."

"How long is temporary?"

"I don't know. My long-term goal is to buy a new house, but I'll probably have to wait until after my divorce. I need to get everything settled with my finances. I'm assuming Delores will fight to keep the house. If so, I think she has to give me my portion of the equity. I'll need that money to get back on my feet."

"Have you thought about moving back to Washington?"

His eyes narrowed. "Why would I do that?"

"Your support system is there. You could move in with your mom, and you'll have someone there to help you recover. Plus it's expensive to live in a hotel. How long do you think you can keep that up?"

"I don't know. If I stop paying the mortgage at home, it won't be so bad. If I keep paying the mortgage, it'll be hard to pay for a hotel too. But I'm not moving back to Washington. My career is here, and my daughter… And you."

She pursed her lips.

"What will it take to make you feel better?" he wondered.

"I don't know if I can feel better right now. On top of worrying about your health, I'm worried about your new living arrangements. I don't like the idea of you being alone in a hotel, fresh out of the hospital."

"You would rather I be with Delores?"

The anxiety in her eyes was palpable. "No. I don't want that either. Evan, I don't know what I want."

"Are you upset with me for leaving her?"

"No, but I'm still not happy that you did it for me. And now you won't have anyone to..."

She trailed off because of the look in his eyes. His focus had shifted from her to something in the doorway. Now that the room was quiet, Jada heard the sound of someone approaching. She turned and was stunned to see that Sharelle had not only entered the room; she was standing right behind her. Jada wondered how much of their conversation the girl had heard. From the look in her eyes, Jada feared she had heard too much.

"Hi," she said. "I was just giving your dad his discharge orders. I already called transport to come take him down."

Sharelle didn't respond. Her eyes were cold and disbelieving. Jada's heart froze. Her body went numb.

"Okay, I'll let you two be alone," she said and made a hasty retreat.

Sharelle waited until they were in the car, on the way to the hotel, before she confronted her father. Evan knew there was trouble brewing. She hadn't spoken much when they were inside his room, waiting for the transporter. When they got in her car, he noticed Sharelle's death grip on the steering wheel. She maintained a hard stare on the road, rather than look over at him.

"Daddy, how could you?"

Like Jada, he wasn't sure how much she'd overheard when she walked into his room. Until he knew for sure, denial seemed like the best option.

"What are you talking about?"

"You and that nurse are having an affair! I knew it was something going on with y'all!"

His blood ran cold. "Wha, why would you say that?"

She looked his way then. Her eyes brimmed with tears and betrayal.

"I heard what she said to you! Why are you denying it?"

"Okay, you need to lower your voice. I don't know what you think–"

"Why are you lying?!"

She was so upset, spittle flew from her mouth. Though Evan knew he was wrong, there were certain things he would not tolerate.

"I asked you to lower your voice. I don't care how upset you are, you're not gonna yell at me, like I'm one of your friends from school."

His voice was calm, but his eyes were hard, his features reminiscent of the stern talks he'd given her when she was younger. As was the case when she was a child, Sharelle cracked under the pressure. Tears spilled from her eyes.

"I know you're having an affair with her," she cried. *"She said you were leaving mom for her."*

Now that he knew what she had heard, Evan racked his brain for a way to counter it. He couldn't come up with anything.

"I'm not leaving your mom because of her."

"Dad, please stop–"

"Let me finish."

She piped down, other than the sounds of her crying, the hitching of her sorrow-filled breaths.

"I would like to start a relationship with Jada after I'm divorced," he admitted. "But we're not currently in a relationship." He felt that was technically true, but he understood it was still a lie of omission. "Everything I told you yesterday about why I'm leaving your mother is true. I didn't mention Jada, because she's not a factor in this."

"I heard what she said. Why does she think you're leaving mom for her, if you're not?"

Evan felt cornered. The confines of her Camry never felt so small.

"She feels that way because we discussed being in a relationship, and then I told her I wasn't going home to my wife. It's a natural reaction for her to think I'm leaving my wife for her."

"If you're talking about being in a relationship with someone while you're still married, that means you're having an affair."

He hated that she was so rational. "No, not necessarily."

"*Explain why it's not,*" she cried. "You don't just walk up to some random person and say, '*Hey, would you like to be in a relationship when I divorce my wife.*'"

Evan sighed.

"Dad, you've never been one to lie to me. Why are you doing it now?"

"Because this is complicated, and I don't think you can understand it."

"No, I think you're lying because you know I *do* understand it, and it's not right. You're cheating on Mom, and that's why you want a divorce."

"Alright," he conceded. "If you wanna see it as an affair, I guess you're probably right."

Her face crumbled again as more tears fell.

"But it's not what I would consider an affair. Jada and I haven't gone out on a date, I've never called her at home, we've never slept together or anything like that. All we've done is talk while I was in the hospital."

The lie made him feel like his chest was on fire. Jada had told him how wrong their actions were. Evan didn't feel the full impact of it until it came from his daughter. He was her hero, her biggest role model. Betraying his wife was nothing compared to the anguish he had brought upon his little girl.

She accepted his answer and said, "Then it's an emotional affair."

"If that's what you want to call it," he repeated.

"Tell me what you wanna call it, Dad. You're doing your best to avoid the word *affair*, so tell me what you think is going on with you and your nurse."

Evan recognized the shift in their relationship. It didn't feel like very long ago when he'd force her to admit to a wrong first, before she had to face the consequences. He understood why it was necessary when he did it, but now that the tables were turned, he didn't see why this acknowledgement was needed.

He bit the bullet and said, "I'm having an emotional affair with my nurse."

His daughter banged on the steering wheel as her cries became even louder. Evan watched the road, fearing she might veer into oncoming traffic. His hand was poised to grab the wheel if she did.

"I'm sorry," he told her, "but I wasn't lying about the reasons I'm leaving your mother. Everything I told you yesterday is true. This thing with me and Jada doesn't factor into it."

"Yeah, right. You've been lying so much, I don't think you even know what the truth is anymore."

"Alright," Evan said, with a hard nod of his head. "I'ma let you have this fit, but it's probably better if we don't talk about this anymore. I'm not gon' stand for this disrespect. Even when I'm wrong, I'm still your father, and you will respect me. If you don't feel like you can do that right now, it's best not to say anything at all."

Sharelle took that advice and kept her mouth closed the rest of the way to the hotel. When they got there, she was mindful of the fact that he couldn't lift any of his baggage. She dutifully helped him get everything into his room on the sixth floor. He hoped by then she'd be calm enough to have another discussion about what was going on, but her agony had shifted to anger.

Her features were set in a sneer when she dropped the last bag off in his room. She turned and left him there without saying goodbye.

Jada had been tense since Evan and his daughter left the unit. Trying to get her work done while waiting to find out what happened with Sharelle was almost mission impossible. She checked her cellphone so often, she feared she'd get reprimanded by her charge nurse. Each time she looked, she had not missed a call or text message from Evan. She finally accepted that he was probably waiting until her shift was over, before he called to tell her what happened with him and his daughter.

At five p.m., Jada couldn't say she was surprised when Evan's wife thundered onto the unit like a bat out of hell. She wasn't surprised when Delores stomped straight to the nurses' station, looking around wildly until she spotted Jada and zeroed in on her. She wasn't surprised that Evan's wife didn't bother to fix her hair or put on makeup before rushing to the hospital.

Delores wasn't disheveled, but this was the roughest Jada had ever seen her. Her eyebrows were bunched together. The scowl on her face was deep and menacing.

"You fucking bitch!"

The nurses' station had a large counter that wasn't meant to be a barrier between the staff and the patients, but it could double as one if need be. Jada's fight or flight instincts kicked-in in an instant. She leapt from her seat and made her way around the counter, as Delores invaded their work area.

"You slept with my husband!"

Delores' eyes were wild and demonic. The last time she and Jada had words, the assistant principal put her career ahead of whatever bodily harm she wanted to inflict on the nurse. Today she had no such qualms. She raced through the nurses' station, her hands up, her nails extended like talons. Jada continued to circle the counter, keeping it between herself and the deranged wife. She had no words. Her heart slammed in her chest like a jackhammer.

"Why you running, bitch?!"

Realizing she wasn't as quick as the wily nurse, Delores reached over the counter and then began to climb it. Finally the monitor tech grabbed one of her arms.

"Ma'am, you need to–"

She jerked away from him roughly. *"Get the fuck off me!"*

Percy was 5'10, 240 pounds. He recoiled for a second before grabbing her again. He didn't let go this time.

"Stop!" he shouted. *"What the hell are you doing?"*

Delores' eyes remained focused on the adulterer.

"I'ma kill you, bitch! You know I'ma kill yo ass!"

"What the hell is going on here?" The charge nurse rushed to the nurses' station to help restrain Delores. *"What are you doing back here? Woman, have you lost your mind?"*

"That bitch is sleeping with my husband!" Delores shouted.

There had been so much chaos since Delores showed up on the up on the unit, none of what she was saying fully registered. But her last declaration stopped everything cold. Even Sheila momentarily loosened her grip on Delores' arm as the accusation set in.

"You, she what?"

"She slept with my husband!" Delores yelled. *"Evan Shales!* He just got discharged today. He didn't come home to me, because your nurse is having an affair with him!"

All eyes were on Jada now. She prayed a hole would open in the floor and swallow her. No such luck. She was forced to look all of her coworkers in the eyes and endure their shocked, condemning and mortified stares. Jada couldn't have been more embarrassed if she shit her pants right then and there. Coincidentally, she felt like that might just happen.

"I, you, you..." Sheila struggled to get her words together. "Right now, I don't give a damn if she is," she finally said. "You're not about to attack one of my employees. Melissa, call security."

The tech she was speaking to remained frozen in place, her eyes and mouth wide, looking from the woman's angry face to Jada's, which was filled with guilt.

"Melissa!" Sheila barked.

The tech snapped out of her shock.

"You ain't gotta call security on me!" Delores shouted. "I'll fucking leave! *Let me go!*"

"I'm not letting you go until you're on the elevator, on your way off this unit," Sheila countered. "If you're ready to go, come on. I'll take you myself. Let her go, Percy," she said to the monitor tech.

Percy gave her a questioning look.

"Let her go," Sheila said again, more calmly this time. "I swear, if you make one dumb move," she told Delores, "he's gonna tackle you."

Delores didn't respond. She continued to shoot daggers at Jada with her eyes. She breathed roughly through her nostrils.

Percy released his grip on her other arm, and Delores remained still.

After a second, Sheila said, "Alright, come on," and tried to walk her to the elevator.

Before she complied, Delores told her husband's nurse, "I hope you don't think this is the end of this. I'ma get you fired, you fucking whore! Mark my words. Today's your *last* day working as a nurse."

Jada didn't think Evan's wife had the power to end her career, but she couldn't deny there would be major repercussions for what had just happened. She hadn't said a word since Delores arrived on the unit. She remained mute when the woman finally turned away from her and allowed the charge to lead her off the floor.

CHAPTER FIFTEEN
FIRST DATE

Jada had expected Evan to wait until after her shift before he'd call. She had just gotten into her car when her phone vibrated. She didn't recognize the number on her caller ID.

"Hello?"

"Hi, Jada."

Hearing his voice didn't fill her with euphoria, like it usually would.

"Hi, Evan."

The misery in her voice was transparent.

"What's wrong? What happened?"

She sighed. "You wife came to the hospital a couple of hours ago."

"What?"

"She ran right to the nurses' station and started yelling at me, trying to start a fight."

Evan's eyes widened. He knew Delores had a mean streak. She had threatened a couple of girls when they were in college. Evan recalled her trying to go after one of his exes at a campus party. But she hadn't exhibited that level of rachetness since then. Once she started teaching, she usually carried herself with professionalism.

He said, "Are you serious?"

"Yeah. I think I'm gonna get in trouble."

"Why? Why would you get in trouble for something she did?"

"She made a huge scene," Jada explained. The sound of her voice was robotic. All the explaining she'd had to do since Delores was escorted off the unit left her numb. Her body and mind welcomed the opportunity to get home and shut down for the day.

"She told everyone I was having an affair with you," she continued. "She called me a bunch of names, cursing. She really tried to get a hold of me. She was running around, completely wild. It took two people to restrain her. I've been at the hospital for a long time. We've had fights with employees before. But I've never seen anything like that with a guest and a staff member. I've never even heard of it."

"Oh my God. I'm so sorry that happened to you."

"It's alright. It's not your fault."

"I feel like it is. Are you gonna be alright? Did she hurt you?"

"No, she never touched me. I took off the moment I saw her coming. She was gonna kick my ass. Bad enough she told everyone what was happening with us. I didn't need to get my ass kicked on top of that."

"Jesus, this is... Damn, Jada. This is fucked up."

"Yup," she said with a nod. "It's most definitely fucked up."

"Where are you? Are you headed home?"

"Yeah. I'm tired. I can't take no more stress today. Going to sleep is the only way to make this crazy day end."

Evan knew he was being selfish, but he said, "I wanna see you. Can you come to my hotel? We can go have dinner."

Jada checked the clock on her dash. It was only 7:15. She felt like she could go straight to bed, but it was still early. She didn't have an appetite, but seeing Evan might make her feel a little better.

"Okay," she told him. "Text me the address."

Evan's room at the Holiday Inn was neat and cozy. He had already unpacked most of his things, settling in for the long haul. When he opened the door and saw the hopeless, fatigued look in Jada's eyes, his heart bled for her. He pulled her into his embrace and held her tightly, hoping to transfer his strength and resolve to her.

"I feel horrible about all of this," he said, speaking into the top of her beautiful mane. "You are such a wonderful person. You don't deserve this."

Jada didn't know if that was true. She had allowed herself to fall in love with a patient, and she was an active participant in their adultery. She may have been merely complicit in their ill-advised kiss. But what happened in the shower was all her doing.

"This is all my fault," Evan said.

She backed away from him and reached to caress the side of his face. "No, it's not. We're both responsible for what we did."

His eyes filled with tears. He shook his head. "No. You tried to do the right thing. You kept telling me it was wrong. You didn't want to hear me complain about my wife. But I kept pushing. And now everyone at work is going to think differently about you. That's all on me."

A tear spilled from his eye. She was quick to wipe it away.

"Everyone at the hospital respects you," he said. "On the night shift, whenever I tell someone you're my nurse, they always have good things to say about you. They tell me you're one of the best nurses on the unit, and you should be the charge. I couldn't live with myself if Delores ruined that for you."

Jada was surprised to hear the staff on nightshift held her in such high regards, considering she rarely worked with them.

"It's okay, Evan. It's just another hospital scandal." She forced a smile. "Believe me, we've had plenty. In a week or so, they'll move on to the next thing."

"Really?"

She could tell he was eager to grasp onto any hope she was offering. She doubted if Delores' accusations would blow over that easily. But at the moment, her need for Evan to feel better overrode her own distress.

"I'm sure of it," she said.

He nodded. "I hope you're right."

"You said something about dinner," she said. "What did you have in mind?"

He grinned. "I can't believe we're going on a real date. I don't care where we go, as long as I'm with you."

She smiled too. "This *is* our first date, isn't it? What do you like to eat, when you're not at the hospital?"

"I love steak, but—"

"Yeah, you know you can't eat that right now."

"Have you ever been to Salata?" he asked. "It's quick and easy, and it's really good. I can eat healthy there."

"Ooh, I love that place!"

At the restaurant, Evan avoided his usual salad favorites, like the Asian barbeque chicken and falafel. Instead he selected seafood mix with blue cheese crumbles. Jada topped her salad sensibly as well. They made small talk, staring over their plates like school kids.

"It feels so good to be with you outside of the hospital," he told her. "I dreamed this day would come, but I was starting to think it never would."

"I didn't think it would either," she said. "It feels a little weird to not be standing over your hospital bed. I know you're glad to be off my floor."

"I am. I hope I never go back."

"Have you talked to your daughter since she dropped you off."

He frowned. "No. I haven't called her. I don't know what I'm gonna say to her; I'm so pissed."

"Don't be so hard on her."

"Why not? It's her fault Delores showed up on your unit. I know she's the one who called her."

"I don't think she did it to hurt you."

"Maybe not, but she definitely did it to hurt you. She knew her mom would go up there starting shit. She basically sicced her on you."

"Yes, she did. But you have to look at it from her perspective. Her parents are getting a divorce. That's devastating, even for a child her age. And I'm the reason for it."

He shook his head. "No. I keep telling you that's not true. I was gonna leave Delores anyway."

"Evan, you can say that all you want. But we need to be honest with ourselves. If you were gonna leave your wife, you would've done it. You said your relationship has been rocky for years."

"But it didn't become a huge problem until I got sick. That's when her true colors started to show."

"That's also when you developed feelings for me. At the very least, you have to admit that I pushed you to do something you were already thinking about doing."

"I can accept that."

"Then you have to accept that I'm the cause of you leaving your wife. I don't want to acknowledge that any more than you do. But it's the truth."

He nodded. "Alright."

"Your daughter is hurting. She thinks you're wrong for what you're doing. She thinks I'm even more wrong, because I'm your nurse. She's lashing out at the person she feels is responsible. You have to forgive her and apologize and try to make things right."

He was quiet for a few seconds. "How do I make it right?"

She shrugged. "I don't know, Evan. Going back to your wife would be the easiest solution."

"I'm not doing that," he said quickly.

"The only other thing you can do is man up to your mistake and continue to love her. Sharelle's wounds will heal over time. Getting upset with her will only make it worse."

"Yeah," he said. "You're right. I'll, uh, I'll find some way to fix it."

"I know you will. You're a good man, but even good people make mistakes."

He stared into her eyes. "Jada, I don't believe we're a mistake. Leaving my wife is not a mistake either."

She grinned. "You make me feel so special."

He reached across the table and took her hand. "I'm just returning the favor."

On the way back to the hotel, Evan received a phone call. He grunted when he saw who it was.

Jada looked over at him. "What's wrong?"

"It's Delores. I wonder what the hell she wants."

Jada's body heated. Even though Evan considered himself separated, she still felt like they were cheating.

"Are you gonna answer it?"

"I don't know. Do you think I should?"

She swallowed. "Yeah. It might be important."

"Okay. I'ma put her on speaker."

"You don't have to do that."

"I want to. Anything she has to say to me, she can say in front of you." He grudgingly accepted the call. "Yeah, what's going on?"

His wife said, "I need to talk to you."

He looked Jada's way. She tried to keep her eyes on the road.

"Okay," he said, "I'm listening."

Delores said, "I need to talk to you face to face."

"I don't think that's a good idea."

"Why? Is that *bitch* over at your hotel?"

The heat in Jada's face intensified. Evan's features hardened.

He said, "No."

"Then why don't you want me to come?"

"Because I don't feel like arguing with you anymore. I just got out of the hospital. I'm not supposed to be under any kind of stress."

"You know Sharelle told me where you are, right?"

Evan didn't doubt that. His daughter had been doing a lot of talking lately.

He said, "And...?"

"And you can invite me to your room, or I can show up at your room," Delores said. "Either way, I'm gonna see you tonight."

Evan looked Jada's way. She shrugged and then nodded.

"Alright," he said. "Come to the hotel if you want to. But please don't come with a bunch of drama."

"You're the one having an affair, but you don't want me to come with drama? You got some nerve," she said and disconnected.

When they got to the hotel, Jada's feelings of being the other woman kicked into high gear. She was dropping off a man, who may or may not be her boyfriend, so that he could spend time with his wife. She couldn't even walk him to his room, because for all they knew, Delores might already be there waiting for him.

"Do you want to hang out for a while," he asked her. "I'm sure this won't take long."

Jada shook her head. "No. The last thing I need is for her to see me over here."

"You could wait in the parking lot."

Evan didn't know how much she felt like a mistress, so she didn't fault him for suggesting that. She continued to shake her head. "No, Evan. Go on and take care of what you have to do. You can call me when she leaves."

His eyes were flooded with disappointment. "Okay."

He leaned towards her and then winced and settled back in his seat. She reached over and placed a hand on his chest.

"No twisting or bending," she reminded him.

He grinned. "Yes, ma'am."

She leaned towards him instead, and they kissed slowly, softly. Despite all the turmoil in her life, everything seemed to be at peace when his lips were on hers. His passion fueled her soul, as much as it did the first time they kissed.

But when she backed away, she found herself parked in front of his hotel. He still had to leave her to be with his wife.

"I guess I'll go," he said. "I'll call you when she leaves."

Jada nodded. Evan winced again as he got out of the car. Jada wanted so badly to get out and help him, but because of Delores, she couldn't even do that. She drove away wondering if any of this was worth it.

Evan hadn't been in his room for ten minutes before there was a knock on the door. He answered it and found his dearly beloved standing there. He didn't know what Delores looked like when she went to the hospital earlier that evening, but he could tell she'd taken her appearance into consideration before coming to see him.

Her makeup was flawless, her hair recently styled. She wore heels with a skirt he had always complimented. The skirt clung to her curves mercilessly, accenting her hips and thighs. Evan didn't have to wait until she turned her back to him to know that her ass looked scrumptious in the outfit. She seemed to delight in the way he looked at her.

"You gonna invite me in?"

He stepped aside, and she walked in like a model on the catwalk. Evan couldn't help but watch her. He marveled at the bounce of her luscious booty, but she didn't know that he now had a preference for Jada's slimmer physique. He closed the door and stood there. His wife turned to him.

"You don't wanna sit down?" she asked.

He shook his head. "I don't expect you to be here for very long."

"Baby, you just got out of the hospital. You need to sit down."

Evan took offense to her calling him *baby*. He also didn't like her faux show of concern. "Naw, I'm good."

Delores turned away from him and walked around the room. She returned and said, "So this is where you'd rather live, instead of your beautiful home?"

"I wouldn't say I'd rather live here. I'd prefer to be at home, but this is where I have to be to get away from you."

She scoffed at that. "You make it sound like I did you so bad you can't stand to be around me."

"I can tolerate being around you. But I can't stand to be married to you."

"Why, because you fucking that ugly-ass nurse?"

He shook his head and chuckled slightly.

"What's funny?" she snapped.

"I think it's funny that you can treat me like shit for years, but when I decide to leave, you'd rather blame everyone but yourself."

She propped a hand on her hip. "What have I done to you for years?"

"Not much," he said, "other than pursue your job to the fullest, not caring if I was home alone, what I had for dinner, whether I needed you with me at night, while you were in the other room on your laptop. We haven't slept in the same bed in six months."

"What difference does that make? It's not like we can have sex."

"My doctor never said that."

"You know you can't have sex, not with your heart acting up."

"I think my cardiologist should've been the one to put that limitation on me – not my wife. And we don't have to make love to sleep in the same bed. Did it ever cross your mind that I might want to hold you at night? Did you ever want to hold me?"

"I've been sleeping in Sharelle's room so I wouldn't keep you up, Evan. You know that. Sometimes I'm on my laptop 'til one, two in the morning."

He bristled. "Everything's about work with you, even your excuses for not being a good wife."

"You mad at me because I'm trying to better myself?"

He shook his head. "I'm not mad at you, Delores. I wish nothing but the best for you. But when you're married, you have to have balance. You can't give your profession 90 percent of you and expect your husband to be happy with the remaining ten percent. You haven't treated me like you love me, like I was important to you, for a long time."

"So what are you saying, you want me to give you more of my time?"

"That may have worked before I got sick. But when I needed you the most, that's when you really showed your ass. You complained about the bills, all the procedures I had to do. The last straw was when you didn't want me to have surgery."

"I never said that."

"It was in your eyes. You told Sharelle we should discuss our options."

"What's wrong with that?"

"One option was for me to have a surgery that would add years to my life. The other option was to have a procedure that would give me a few months to live. What kind of wife thinks that's really an option? If you loved me, it wouldn't have been up for discussion. But all you saw was what it would cost us, how our bank accounts would look if we did the surgery.

"You've been complaining about who's gonna take care of me when I can't take out the trash, how our life was gonna be *soooo* fucked up because my heart doesn't work right. Do you know how that makes me feel? I'm fucking *dying*, right before your eyes, and you can't be compassionate enough to make me feel like my life means something to you. You are so goddamned selfish. All you care about is how my problems are gonna effect you.”

Delores' eyes blazed. “If you're so fucking sick, why would you turn around and fuck your nurse? Do you know how that makes me look? Do you know how embarrassing that is?”

He smiled at that.

“*What's so funny*?”

“It's funny because your head is so far stuck up your ass, you're proving my point, and you don't even know it.”

“What are you talking about?”

“You're not hurt because of what I did. You haven't shed one single tear. You're mad because a woman as awesome as you can't stand to lose her husband to another woman. You're mad because I'm making you look bad. It's still all about you, because you're the only person you care about.”

She appeared stunned but didn't bother denying what he said. She nodded angrily.

“Alright, well I want you to know I went up to that bitch's job today. I told everyone what y'all are doing. I'ma make sure she loses her job.”

Evan didn't respond.

“If you divorce me,” she continued, “I hope you know you're not getting shit when the cause of divorce is *adultery*. I'm keeping the house, the savings, all our property. The only thing you're gonna have is your car and whatever clothes you want to pack up. I'm gonna *ruin* you.”

Evan shrugged.

“And I'm not paying any more of your medical bills,” she said. “Good luck starting over with all this debt hanging over you. And I hope you know you destroyed your relationship with your daughter. Sharelle will never forgive you for what you did. She used to look up to you. You could never do wrong in her eyes. Not anymore. She hates you, just as much as I do."

He gave her a bored expression. "Are you through?"

The sneer that formed on the right side of her face was so deep, he wondered if it would get stuck that way.

"Yeah, I'm through, Evan. Good luck with your miserable, little life and your unemployed bitch. You're gonna need it."

She stomped towards him. Evan opened the door for her and locked it when she passed through.

He had managed to maintain composure while she was in the room, but the weight of their argument took its toll when she was gone. He took a seat on the sofa and stared at the blank television screen until the room became a blur. He didn't realize he was crying until he felt the tears rolling down his cheeks.

He dug his phone from his pocket and wiped his eyes, so he could read the display. He accessed his recent calls and cleared his throat before Jada answered.

"Hey," she said. "How'd it go?"

"Umm..." He sighed. "As well as to be expected. She hates me, and she says my daughter hates me too. She's gonna make it her mission to ruin both of us. Other than that, it went great."

"Your daughter doesn't hate you. She's upset with you, but it'll be alright."

"Yeah. Maybe."

"Are you okay?"

"I, uh... I was wondering if you can come back to the hotel. I really wanna be with you right now."

After a pause, she said, "Evan, I'm almost home. I've had a rough day. We both have. I think it's better if we get some rest."

Evan swallowed his emotions, not wanting her to know how badly his heart was breaking. "Okay," he said. "Get some sleep. I'll talk to you tomorrow."

CHAPTER SIXTEEN

POLICIES & LEGALITIES

Jada was off the next day. Her heart dropped to the pit of her stomach when she received a call from her manager.

"Hello?"

"Hi, Jada. This is Tiffany. I need to speak to you. Would it be alright if you come to my office today?"

Working the day shift, Jada had frequent encounters with her manager, but rarely was she asked to come to her office. Anything Tiffany had to say to her could usually take place on the floor.

"Um, okay," she said. "Can I ask what this is in regard to?"

"Yes, I'm told there was some sort of disturbance at work last night."

"Yeah, there was. I'm sorry."

"It's okay, but we have to discuss it, before I can allow you to come back to work."

Jada stared wide eyed at her bedroom wall. "Alright. Is, is this not something we can discuss right now?"

"No, I'm sorry, Jada, but I need to see you in person. It won't take that long."

"Okay. Is it alright if I talk to you when I come back to work on Wednesday?"

"I really need to take care of this today."

"Okay... I can be there in an hour."

"Great. It's nine o'clock. So you'll be here at ten?"

"Yeah, around that time."

"Come at ten," Tiffany said. "I'm going to be away from the floor, but I'll make sure I'm here at ten."

"Alright. I'll see you then."

Jada took a shower and dressed slowly. It only took her fifteen minutes to get to the hospital. She didn't want to get there early, because Tiffany had been specific, almost adamant about the meeting starting at ten o'clock. Jada had been working at the hospital long enough to know what that meant. This had never happened to her, but she knew of plenty others.

When she arrived on her unit, she had to do the walk of shame to her manager's office. All eyes were on her, but no one stopped her to ask questions. A few said hello. Most just looked. Some averted their attention when she made eye contact with them.

Tiffany's door was open. Jada walked inside and was not surprised to see another woman seated at the desk. The newcomer had positioned her chair on Tiffany's side, presumably so they could create a united front. Jada checked the stranger's ID badge. She sucked air between her teeth when saw that she was from Human Resources.

"Hi, Jada," Tiffany said. "Close the door and have a seat."

Jada closed the door, but she didn't want to sit down. She hesitated, a bit too long. Both ladies stared at her in the interim. Jada finally took the seat across from the two ladies. Her face was deadpan, as was "Sherri's" from human resources. Tiffany offered a smile.

"How are you?" Tiffany asked.

"Okay," Jada replied, "other than feeling like I'm being set up."

"Oh, no. This isn't a setup," Tiffany said. "Sherri had to come down to deal with some of the technical stuff I don't know about."

"Hi, Jada," Sherri said and proceeded to take over the meeting. "Do you want to tell me what happened last night?" She had a laptop open on Tiffany's desk. Her fingers were poised to type whatever Jada said.

"A woman came to the hospital and tried to start a fight with me," Jada stated.

Sherri typed.

"Do you know the woman?" she asked.

"Yes. She's the wife of one of my patients. He was discharged yesterday."

More typing.

"What is the patient's name?"

"Evan Shales."

"Do you know why the woman was upset with you?"

Jada's chest shuddered. "She accused me of having an affair with her husband."

"Okay. Are you having an affair with her husband?"

"No."

"Have you ever gone out with him?"

"Prior to him being discharged, no."

"What about after that?"

"Yes. I saw him last night."

More typing. Tiffany didn't let on how she felt about any of this.

"Have you ever kissed him, prior to him being discharged yesterday?" Sherri asked.

Jada's hesitation was all the answer they needed, but she said, "Yes."

Tiffany could barely contain her gasp.

"Have you had sex with him, prior to him being discharged yesterday?"

Jada shook her head. "No."

"Any inappropriate touching."

Jada hesitated again before saying, "Yes."

"Did the kiss and inappropriate touching happen while he was admitted at this hospital?"

By then, Jada knew she was getting fired. She said, "Yes."

Sherri nodded. "Are you aware of page 56, section two of your employee handbook."

Jada shook her head.

"It deals with romantic relationships between staff and patients. I'll read it to you..."

She began reading so quickly, Jada knew she already had it pulled up on her computer, which confirmed her belief that this had been a setup all along.

"Romantic and/or sexual relationships between staff and patients are generally abuse of power violations by staff, based on the patient's need for care. Staff members are likely to be viewed as power figures that provide care for patients regardless of being a direct treatment provider or not. Such relationships are prohibited and will be viewed as staff-patient boundary violations that have resulted in an unethical relationship."

Jada had vaguely heard of that policy. She didn't respond.

"In light of what you've told us," Sherri said, "I'm afraid we have to suspend you, pending further investigation. Tiffany tells me you're a great employee, and other than this incident, you haven't had any writeups in the past year."

"I've never had a writeup," Jada interjected.

Sherri continued speaking, as if she hadn't heard her. "We will take your manager's recommendation into consideration as well as your annual evaluations and years of service before we make our final decision on termination. Did you bring your badge with you? I have to confiscate it, until we get everything figured out."

The hospital ID badges not only served to identify employees. They were skeleton keys that unlocked all proxy doors in the hospital, with the exception of floors on Labor and Delivery and a few other highly secured areas. Jada knew the IT department could disable any proxy card at any time, but former employees had been known to use old ID's to pose as active employees, sometimes for nefarious reasons.

Jada removed her ID badge from her purse. She handed it to the woman, knowing she would never see it again.

She drove in a trance when she left the hospital. She was hardly aware of where she was going until she pulled into the parking lot of Evan's hotel. Before she got out of the car, it occurred to her that she didn't know his room number and he might have company. She dug her phone from her purse and called him.

"Hey, Jada?"

"Yeah. I, um, I'm outside your hotel. Are you busy?"

"No. I'm glad you came. After last night, I was worried I wouldn't see you again."

"Why do you say that?"

"You sounded kinda cold, like you were rethinking this – having second thoughts about us."

"I was," she admitted.

"I'm sorry to hear that. What changed your mind?"

"I slept on it, and when I woke up this morning, I decided that I'm going to trust my heart, no matter what. My dedication to you was tested two hours later, but I still want to be with you."

Her words made Evan's soul glow, but then he considered her full statement. "Your dedication was tested? What do you mean by that?"

"What's your room number?" she asked. "I'll explain when I get up there."

She entered his room a few minutes later and found the smell of fresh coffee reminiscent of the road trips she used to take with her family. Evan greeted her wearing a short-sleeved button down with jeans. After a warm embrace, he asked if she wanted something to drink.

"I'll have some water."

She watched him as he got it for her. She was surprised that his movements were almost back to normal.

She asked, "Where's the walker they sent you home with?"

"It's in the bedroom."

"You haven't been using it?"

"I have. I have to use it to get out of bed sometimes. But when I'm sitting in here, I can use the arm of the sofa. I used it when I took a shower last night, 'cause I don't have a shower chair."

The thought of him in the shower made Jada blush as she sat down. Evan seemed to notice as he took a seat across from her.

"What are you thinking about?" he asked with a grin.

"Nothing," she said, grinning too.

"Do you think one day we'll be able to talk about that shower you helped me with?"

She brought a hand to her mouth, chuckling. "Maybe one day. I'm still embarrassed about it. That's, um..." Her smile faded. "That's what I wanted to talk to you about."

Confused, he said, "Hmm? What's up?"

She sighed, cradling her water bottle in both hands. "They called me to the hospital today and suspended me. I'm pretty sure I'm fired, they just haven't said so yet."

His eyes widened. "What? Why?"

"Because of what your wife told them last night. I knew they weren't gonna let me off with a slap on the wrist."

"But last night you said it was no big deal, just another scandal."

"I said that because I didn't want to upset you. I kinda knew I was gonna get fired."

"Why would they fire you for something Delores did? It's not your fault she made a scene."

"It's against hospital policy for a staff member to have a relationship with a patient. It didn't matter if it was an affair. Any type of relationship is considered inappropriate."

Evan continued to stare at her. "Why didn't you deny it? We've never gone out or anything."

"If I would've denied it, they would've contacted Delores and asked why she felt that way, and then they would've contacted Sharelle and asked why she felt that way. And then they would've asked everyone on the unit what they knew about it. My name would've been drug through the mud for a whole week. I'm done lying about it, Evan. Our relationship is founded on deceit, and that's not who I am. I'm trying to turn the page and be forthcoming from now on."

Evan's feature's contorted, as if he was staring at a dying child, and then he buried his face in his hands.

"Oh my God, Jada. I'm so sorry. This is the worst thing that could've happened. This is all my fault. What have I done? I cost you everything!"

She rushed to his sofa and sat next to him. She wrapped both arms around his torso and lay her head on his shoulder.

"It's okay, Evan."

"No, it's not. You don't have to say that. You've been at that hospital for twenty-something years."

"And I fell in love with a man who was worth throwing it all away."

He gradually lowered his hands and looked her way. "You, you're in love with me?"

Since her divorce, Jada had never uttered those words to another man. With Evan, she wasn't afraid to bare her soul. She nodded. "Yes, Evan. I am."

The elation that flooded him was almost enough to make him forget about her terrible news.

His features were still set in a frown when he said, "I love you too, Jada."

She smiled. She leaned forward and kissed him softly, slowly. She savored the magic in his touch, his lips. Her eyes were moist when she backed away. Evan mistook her happiness for distress.

"It's gonna be alright," he promised her. "I know things are starting off rocky, but we'll make it through this. I hired a lawyer this morning. She's gonna get started on the paperwork for me to file for divorce. She said the date of my legal separation will be the day I moved out of the house."

"Really?" Jada said.

"Yup," he said, smiling. "That means I'm technically single."

She grinned. "No, sir. But it's a start." She lowered her eyes. "There are some things I wanna do with you, when you *do* become single."

He raised an eyebrow. "Really? Like what?"

She laughed. "I'm just kidding."

"Naw, this ain't no laughing matter."

"Evan, you know your heart's not up for it."

"Naw, I'm good! I'm *strong like bull!*"

She laughed even harder. "Maybe we'll see about that someday. In the meantime, what are you doing today?"

He shook his head. "Not a thing. Dr. Davi didn't put me on bedrest. I would love to get out of here."

"My schedule is open too. You interested in spending the day with your girlfriend? We gotta celebrate you getting your paperwork started."

His smile was deep and lovely. "I would absolutely love that."

They went downtown and had lunch at On the Border. Jada knew her man was craving steak but was unable to indulge in a full portion. They compromised on a serving of steak and shrimp fajitas, which they shared.

When they were done, Jada asked him, "Are you stuffed?"

He shook his head. "No. I could eat more."

"Perfect," she said. "Small servings."

"I see you're still my nurse," he noticed.

"I'll always be your nurse."

He smiled at that.

They brought his walker, but Evan thought he could walk at least thirty minutes before growing fatigued. Jada was hesitant to walk so far away from her car, where his walker was stored in the trunk. But if worse came to worse, she knew she could assist him back to the vehicle with his arm draped over her shoulder. She'd done it plenty of times at the hospital. His height and weight wouldn't be too much of a hinderance.

They strolled the downtown streets hand in hand. It felt so good to be out in the public with him. They admired the storefronts and the architecture. Jada didn't realize how far they'd walked, until they came upon a bridge that led to the acclaimed Overbrook Meadows Water Gardens. It was then that Evan told her he needed to take a break. Concerned, she checked to see if he was sweating or having trouble breathing. He wasn't.

"I'm okay," he assured her. "Let me just lean on this rail for a second."

She continued to eye him warily as he backed towards the rail.

"Stop it," he told her. "I'm alright. Come here."

She stepped towards him, and he wrapped his arms around her waist. She smiled as she placed her head on his chest and he nuzzled the top of her head with his chin. The sight, sound and smell of the water around them was breathtaking. Jada thought the moment was picture perfect. Neither of them whipped out a camera, but the scene would forever be immortalized in their hearts and minds.

"What's next?" Evan asked when he was ready to resume their promenade.

"I don't know. You wanna catch a movie?"

He smiled. "Yeah, and we can have dinner afterwards..."

"I'm up for that."

"You're gonna stay with me all day?"

"Unless you don't want me to."

"No, I do. I don't ever want you to leave."

The feature they selected was a rom-com that was corny, funny and predictable, but they both loved it, especially when the lovebirds made up at the end and lived happily ever after.

Evan talked her into getting takeout for dinner. His excuse was they could watch another movie in his hotel while they ate. Jada felt he was trying to keep her all day *and* all night, but she didn't protest. She didn't want their enchanting day to end any more than he did.

After watching Bad Boys 2 at his hotel and most of the Tonight Show, she told him he should get some rest.

"You're still healing," she said. "Most of that takes place when you're asleep and not moving around."

"But what if I get sick while you're gone?" he asked.

"Do you feel sick now?"

"No."

"Evan, are you asking me to stay the night?"

His eyes were dead serious as he nodded.

Jada didn't respond. Her eyes were equally serious as she stood and walked to the bedroom. Evan's eyes were on her the whole time. He didn't rise from his seat and follow until she was completely out of sight.

Making love wasn't a foregone conclusion, given Evan's heart condition and the reservations Jada had about offering her most precious gift. They lie in bed fully clothed, kissing, snuggling, enjoying the closeness, the feel of their arms and legs intertwined.

She asked if Evan needed her to change the gauze on his chest. He didn't speak, but he sat up in bed and unbuttoned his shirt.

She told him, "I think you should shower first."

He nodded and scooted to the edge of the bed. She stood and offered a hand to help him up. He took it, but he didn't need much support. He made it to the bathroom on his own and turned on the water. Jada stood outside the bathroom door while he undressed. When she heard him step inside the tub, she returned to the bed to wait on him. But he called her name thirty seconds later.

She stepped into the bathroom and saw that the shower had a glass door, rather than a curtain. The sight of Evan's nude, soapy physique awakened a part of her that had been dormant for months. She licked her lips subconsciously.

"When we were out today," he said, "I forgot to tell you I still need a back scrubber. I meant to buy one."

Her grin was mischievous. "You forgot, huh?"

"I swear I'm not asking for a repeat of last time. I tried to wash my back last night by myself, but it required twisting, and I know you don't want me to do that."

"No, I don't."

"You don't have to get in the tub with me, if you... Oh."

He turned her way and remained fully enthralled as she removed her jumper. Her eyes remained glued to his. Her attention moved southward when she removed her bra and slipped out of her panties. Sure enough, his dick grew by degrees. He was rock hard by the time she was fully nude.

"Damn," he muttered. "Your body is amazing."

Jada sometimes felt self-conscious about her thin physique, but Evan made her feel like she was the finest woman on the planet. He faced her when she stepped into the shower with him. He kissed her more passionately than he ever had. His large hands swam across her hot skin until they found a home on her ass. He grabbed both cheeks and drew her nearer, until they were chest to chest, and the feel of his erection pressed against her sent a wave of ecstasy down her frame. The juices she felt between her legs had nothing to do with the water from the shower.

After kissing and fondling her for a few breathtaking minutes, he said, "I guess you want me to turn around, so you can wash my back."

Jada didn't have the wherewithal to respond.

He released her and turned, and she marveled at his muscles, the way his back fanned out, his strong shoulders and arms. She found his soap and washcloth and washed him, from his neckline to his backside. She stepped closer and reached around him, so she could wash his chest. Her touch was delicate on his incision scar, she scrubbed his toned abs normally.

She dropped the soap and reached for his manhood with both hands. He was still unbelievably hard. She knew he was ready to blow. She squeezed and caressed him briefly, not wanting him to climax.

"We need to get out of this tub," she whispered, "before we make a mess in here."

"Okay," he said. "But you didn't let me wash your back yet, or your front."

She shook her head when he turned to her. She told him, "If you put your hands on me like that, I don't think I could take it."

He smiled. "Let's find out."

She bent to retrieve the soap and washcloth she'd discarded. On the way back up, she found herself face to face with a sight that was so enticing, she couldn't stop herself from taking him into her mouth. Evan's eyes widened as she sucked him down. Jada's eyes slipped closed. It didn't take long before the feel of him pulsating in her mouth made her salivate. Once again, she stopped before he erupted. She stood and stared into his dreamy, lust-filled eyes.

Her expression became serious when she said, "I want to make love to you Evan, but I'm afraid."

He nodded. "I know you are. But hey, if I have a heart attack while we're making love, I'll die with a smile on my face."

"That's not funny. I'm serious."

"I am too."

She grinned. "So you get to die with your smile stuck on sex face, and I have to live with the memory of what happened? That's not a fair trade."

"Just roll me off of you and tell everyone I passed in my sleep," he suggested.

"I'm not letting you get on top, Evan. You'd have to exert way too much energy."

"I would love it if you got on top."

She laughed. "I've never negotiated sex before. This is weird."

"But you agreed to it?"

"Yeah, I guess so. I can't have you going to sleep with your dick this hard. That wouldn't be healthy."

His hand slipped between her legs unexpectedly. She gasped when one of his fingers slid easily between her labia.

"And I can't have you going to sleep this wet," he said. "As *your* nurse, I would say that's also unhealthy."

Before they left the shower, he bathed her fully, and Jada somehow found the strength to leave the bathtub on her own accord. Her legs were so weak, she wobbled more than walked to the front room to find her purse. She found a condom that surprisingly wasn't expired.

When she returned to the bedroom, Evan lie on his back, his dick sticking up like a lead pipe. He propped himself up on his elbows and watched her enter.

He shook his head dreamily and said, "Turn around."

Confused, she asked, "Why?"

"I wanna see your ass again."

Her face heated. "My ass isn't that big."

"I love your ass. I could stare at it for days."

She turned, long enough for him to get his peek. When she faced him again, she could tell that he truly appreciated every inch of her body.

"Is it okay if I turn off the lights now?"

He nodded.

In the darkness, Evan felt a myriad of sensations and emotions, all of which deepened his affection for the nurse he'd fallen in love with, long before he expressed those sentiments.

The feel of her mouth on his meat was just as pleasing as it was in the shower. He had to fight against his own natural desires and curl every one of his toes to stop himself from cumming. When she slid the condom on and eased down onto him, he thought he very well could die right then – not because of any discomfort in his chest, but from an overload of pleasure and joy, the likes of which he'd never known.

She rode him like a midnight wave, and he held onto her ass for dear life, and he felt her cum, both times. Only then did he allow himself to explode inside her.

When the pulses of his ejaculation subsided, she lowered herself until her breasts rested on his chest. Her breath on his lips was sweet and warm.

She kissed him and asked, "Are you okay?"

"I feel better than I ever have."

He felt her walls contract around his erection.

She asked him, "Why are you still so hard?"

He responded, "Why does your pussy feel so good?"

"Do you want me to see if I have another condom?"

He grinned in the darkness. "I swear you be reading my mind."

CHAPTER SEVENTEEN
THE FINAL CHAPTER
EVAN'S HEART

The next morning Jada awakened fully nude, a bright smile on her face. The sunlight from the bedroom window was moderate. She didn't think it was after eight a.m. She took a few deep, satisfying breaths, loving her surroundings, her man, and the scent of their sex, that was still prevalent in the small room.

Thinking about all that had transpired yesterday brought a wistful tear to her eye. She knew her overriding concern should be her job, but whether she was still employed or not was not as prevalent as the happiness Evan had brought her. Nothing seemed to matter when she was with him. She didn't know where her new life would lead her, but she was confident and excited to explore this new chapter with the man of her dreams.

When she reached to wrap an arm around him, she found the sheets draped over his torso was moist and warm. She knew things had been very wet last night, but it was unusual for the sheets to remain that way hours later. Her hand moved up his chest, and she realized it wasn't only the sheets that were wet, it was Evan. She sat up and saw that his face and neck were slick with sweat.

Stunned, she tried to rouse him. "Evan. Evan, are you okay?"

No response.

"Evan..."

She reached for his chin and turned his face towards her. When she released him, his head rolled back to the pillow.

"Evan! Oh my God! Evan!"

Despite the fact that she was screaming in his face, his eyes remained closed, his body lifeless. But she watched his chest and saw that it was rising and falling.

She jumped out of bed, her brain racing, all of her senses rudely awakened. She sprinted to the front room and retrieved her cellphone from her purse. She rushed back to the bedroom and tried to wake him again before she made the call.

"Evan, please, baby. Wake up. *Please.*"

Tears spilled from her eyes as she shook his shoulder and watched his eyes and mouth for any signs of consciousness. There was none.

She was still fully nude when she called 9-1-1.

Evan awakened in a familiar place. Even with the limited view provided from his exam room, he knew he was in the ER at Jackson Memorial. His recollection of what had happened to him was foggy. He vaguely remembered flashing lights of what he assumed was an ambulance, accompanied by Jada's voice. She was by his side telling him everything would be okay and to keep breathing. He remembered bright lights and feeling motionless as he was wheeled into the ER. Other than that, he didn't recall anything.

When he opened his eyes in the exam room, it took a few moments to focus. He realized he was on a stretcher, the sound of a heart monitor beeped steadily somewhere above him, and he was wearing an oxygen mask. He wouldn't describe what he felt in his chest as *pain*, but there was pressure. It felt as if someone had placed a heavy dictionary on his sternum.

He turned his head and saw that he had one visitor. He knew Jada hadn't left his side throughout the ordeal. She sat quietly, stoically, watching him. She rose from her seat and approached the stretcher when she saw that he was awake. He knew she was distraught, but she tried to be strong and offer him a supportive smile, just as she'd done the many times she entered his room on the third floor of the cardiac tower.

"Hey, sleepy head. Did you get a good nap?"

He smiled weakly. He felt completely drained. He wondered how he could have so much energy the day before and feel like this less than twelve hours later.

"What happened?" he asked through the mask.

He could tell that Jada understood him perfectly.

"I don't know," she said with a shake of her head. "When I woke up this morning, you were sweating, and you wouldn't respond. I couldn't get you to wake up, so I called 9-1-1."

Evan's eyes filled with tears. "It's my heart."

His statement didn't require confirmation, but Jada nodded.

"They're still running tests. You were in AFib with RVR when you got here. They got your heart rate down, but you're still going in and out of AFib. Dr. Davi's here. She wants to do an ECHO. They asked me to let them know when you woke up."

"Is it okay," he asked, "you being here, after what happened?"

She shrugged and pursed her lips. Despite her efforts, she couldn't get the forlorn look out of her eyes.

"I'm suspended, but I'm not barred from coming to the hospital as a visitor. It's a little embarrassing, but no one in the ER knows what happened on my floor. If you get sent to C3, I don't know how I'd handle that. I'd still go, but it would be hard to look those people in the eyes, especially my manager."

"I'm sorry."

"We're past that, Evan. I already told you I was willing to take whatever comes with loving you. It won't be any worse than when I got beat up in the 9th grade, and I had to go to school the next day and endure the laughing and bullying."

"That's why you ran away from Delores," Evan said. "You can't fight."

That put a genuine smile on her face. "Oh, you got jokes."

"Gotta laugh to keep from crying."

She reached and wiped the tears that were sliding down his face. "I'll go tell them you're awake, so they can page Dr. Davi."

Evan nodded. "Okay. Thanks for being here with me. All jokes aside, I know it was hard for you to come back to this hospital."

"No," she said, her eyes watering. "Hard was waking up and finding you unresponsive. Running into my former coworkers has nothing on that."

Dr. Davi visited with her patient and then sent Evan for a stat ECHO. They sent him back to his exam room in the ER while she looked over the results. She returned to the room less than an hour later. The look on her face as she approached Evan's stretcher made him wonder if she still believed in him and had faith in his recovery.

"Good afternoon, Evan."

"Hey, doc."

With the fluids they'd been giving him, some of his energy had returned, but he didn't attempt to sit up for her. They'd removed his oxygen mask prior to the ECHO, and thankfully they hadn't put it back on. He was able to speak with her freely.

"Jada, how are you?" Dr. Davi asked her.

"I'm okay," she said.

"I heard about what happened on your unit," the cardiologist said. "It was horrible to hear that. If you need me to speak to someone in Human Resources on your behalf, please let me know."

Jada was surprised and a little confused by the offer. She knew Dr. Davi was a devout Christian. She and Jada had a great relationship, but it seemed odd the doctor would stick her neck out for her under these circumstances.

"Thank you," Jada said, "I appreciate that."

The cardiologist returned her attention to Evan.

"What's the damage?" he asked her. "How bad are things looking now?"

"I wish I had good news," she said, "but your heart disease is progressing rapidly. Another one of your valves is starting to fail you."

Evan couldn't say he was shocked by that news, but it was devastating to know nothing was working. All the procedures, medications and therapy had done nothing but prolong the inevitable. His stomach twisted as the dark hand of death caressed him.

"It's your mitral valve this time," she told him. "Since I've been treating you, your problems have all been on the left side of your heart. This valve is on the right. At this rate, I'm afraid we're headed for full cardiac arrest. I'm sorry, Evan. I thought we were starting to turn the page, but we've now reached a worst-case scenario. We have to accept that your heart is not going to heal on its own, and we have to take drastic measures to save your life."

Evan noticed Jada was crying softly. Despite the devastating news, he resolved to keep his eyes dry, for her sake.

"Does this have anything to do with any strenuous activities I might have done recently?" he asked.

The question was for Jada's sake. He knew she'd blame herself, thinking their lovemaking was the cause of his new cardiac episode. He also knew she wouldn't ask the question herself.

The cardiologist shook her head. "No, Evan. There are no signs of that. This is a progression of your heart disease. We knew it was starting to spread to the right side, but I did not believe it would be this devastating so quickly."

Evan swallowed and nodded. "So, what's next, doc?"

He felt like he'd asked that question a hundred times since he'd known her. Each time he was up for the new challenge. This time, her response took all of the breath from his lungs and made his head spin.

"Evan, you need a new heart. I'm putting you on the transplant list."

He stared at her wide-eyed. His heart, what was left of it, did not beat at all as the full weight of her statement sunk in.

"The heart transplant list is very long," she continued. "Many patients expire before they find a suitable donor. In the meantime, you must have another surgery. You will need a ventricular assist device, a VAD, to keep your heart beating while you're waiting for a donor."

She handed him a pamphlet Evan wasn't aware that she'd been holding. He opened it and saw a picture that made his heart thud sporadically. The illustration showed a patient with an odd and obtrusive mechanical device inside his chest. The device, which was labeled a LVAD pump had three tubes. One disappeared inside the bottom of the heart. The other was inserted in the top of the heart. The third tube exited the patient's side and was connected to a control unit that was worn externally. Each side of the unit had a battery that rested on the patient's sides.

As Evan took in the graphic, he realized his cardiologist didn't say she recommended this procedure or that it was optional. Dr. Davi said he *must* have this surgery. Evan took a deep breath and looked up from the pamphlet.

"Typically," the doctor said, the "VAD can keep a patient's heart pumping for up to ten years. But in your case, as your heart disease continues to progress. I do not believe it will work for half that long. Probably less than three years. I pray that you will find a donor before..."

In all the time he'd been her patient, Evan had never known Dr. Davi to trail off like that. He continued to stare at her, waiting for her to finish the sentence. But she never did.

"I will leave you alone and give you time to read about the procedure and notify your loved ones. Time is of the essence, Evan. If possible, we need to perform this surgery tomorrow."

She turned and left the couple in the room alone. Jada approached the stretcher and took his hands in hers, crying openly. Evan didn't have the words to make her feel better, and at the moment, neither did she. The hospital had never felt so cold.

After a minute, he asked her, "Do you have my phone? I need to call my daughter."

When Sharelle arrived in the ER, her look of concern was overpowered by anger when she saw Jada in the exam room.

Before she could react, Evan told her, "She didn't want to be in here when you got here. I asked her to stay."

Jada stood on the opposite side of Evan's stretcher. She watched Sharelle's reaction but didn't speak.

"*What's going on?*" Sharelle asked. Her eyes registered a myriad of emotions. "*Dad, what's happening. Why are you back in the ER? And why is **she** here?*"

"I'm back in the ER because my heart is failing me." He spoke calmly. His eyes were compassionate. "Jada's here because I want her to be."

"You're divorcing mom for her. *Why are you doing this*?"

The girl was near tears, on the verge of a complete meltdown. Evan didn't know if he could be the healer, father and therapist he needed to be at the moment. But he felt he would lose everything if he failed.

"Sharelle, I know you're upset with me. You think I cheated on your mother with this woman, and I'm not going to deny that anymore. I fell in love with Jada while I was married to your mother, and I know that's wrong. That's the worst thing a husband can do to his wife. I've failed you. And I failed your mother. I know it, and I'm sorry.

"I gave you the reasons why I can't be with your mom anymore, but I understand why you want to take it out on Jada. But you need to know that she cared for me at a time when I was very unhappy with my marriage. She not only did her best to care for me as a nurse. She made me feel like I was worth something, when your mom didn't. Jada made me smile when your mom's visits left me heartbroken.

"I told you I didn't want to get into the details of what your mother did to me. I'm still not going to do that. But you have to trust me when I tell you Delores hurt me in a way no other woman ever has. I couldn't stay with her. And Jada has made me happy when no one else could. I love this woman, and she's not going anywhere. I need you to know that."

Sharelle's breaths were visible and heated. She looked from her father to Jada. Her glare was so searing, Jada wanted to avert her eyes, but she didn't look away.

"I have to have another surgery," Evan told his daughter. "But it's just a temporary fix." Despite all efforts to exude strength and confidence, his eyes welled with tears. "The truth is, I need a new heart, baby girl. If I don't get one, I'm gonna die soon. And I... I can't bear the thought of leaving this earth with you mad at me. I need you."

He reached and took her hand. Within seconds, their fingers were interlocked. "I need both of you," he said, looking Jada's way. He reached with his other hand and found hers.

As his first tear fell, he told Sharelle, "I love you baby girl. I'm so sorry I hurt you."

Her floodgate of emotions released as well. Her face crumpled as tears rolled down her cheeks. *I love you too, Daddy. I'm sorry for what I did. I want you to be happy.*

"*You* make me happy," he told her. "You always have, baby girl. Always."

EPILOGUE
TWO YEARS LATER

The sun was just starting to dip in the horizon at Trinity Park on the west side of Overbrook Meadows, but with the pleasant August weather, the area was still teeming with cyclists, kite fliers, families and children at play. The park had a looping biking trail that stretched for miles and a well-worn hiking trail that dipped between hulking maple and pecan trees that were so dense, they completely blocked the sunlight in some areas.

The park had 33 acres of rolling hills with multiple duck ponds, elaborate fountains and numerous picnic areas. The area was best known for hosting Tarrant County's annual kidney walk and the Mayfest, which brought thousands of locals and travelers who enjoyed crafts, rides, musical guests and delicious treats, rivaling the State Fair of Texas in Dallas.

Evan and Jada strolled the wide sidewalk as they neared the final stretch of their walk that would lead them from the park and into their neighborhood on the outskirts of the TCU campus.

Jada wore yoga pants with a form fitting tank top and new sneakers. Evan was equally sporty in a similarly colored tank top and athletic shorts. As was their custom, when they were a half a mile from the end of their walk, he picked up the pace. Jada followed suit. Their speed walking typically escalated to light jogging as they neared the finish line. That evening, Evan surprised her by speeding up even more.

"Oh, you trying to show out," Jada said as she increased her speed and caught up with him.

Jogging side by side, the sound of their sneakers on the pavement was almost in unison. Evan shot her a grin before taking off again. Not to be outdone, Jada sped up as well. She marveled at her man's smooth strides when she pulled alongside him a second time. Their light jogging had become light running. Evan's strong arms and legs cut the air rhythmically. He wasn't sweating yet, and his breathing wasn't labored.

Despite the physical exertion, his tone was conversational when he looked over at her and said, "You know you can't outrun me, right?"

Before she could respond, he took off once again. He exited the park and was full-out sprinting as he rounded the corner into their neighborhood. Try as she might, Jada could not catch up with him before he reached the last two blocks. But it was actually her preference to watch him from behind. Seeing him so physically powerful was exhilarating, as if she was watching an Olympic race. Knowing how far he'd come to reach this level of athleticism put a delighted smile on her face.

He stopped at the next street and turned to wait on her.

"Come on, Grandma. I know you ain't gon' let me do you like that," he said, laughing and panting.

While it was true Jada's oldest child had been blessed with a new addition to the family a few months ago, Evan knew she had not yet become comfortable with the *grandma* label.

"Oh, you are so funny," she said. She slowed and then stopped running when she reached him.

They stood watching each other, both sweating as they caught their breath.

"How long has it been since you ran like that without ending up in the ER?" she teased.

He laughed. "Probably about ten years."

She thought his smile was dazzling.

He turned and continued walking to their home. The TCU neighborhood was historic, but a lot of the homes in the area had been renovated or completely demolished due to gentrification. Jada and Evan were lucky to purchase a new home in the neighborhood during a mortgage crisis. A year after their investment, the appraisal value of their three bedroom flat jumped $30,000, and it was still on the rise.

"If I did have to go to the ER," Evan said, "would you want me to go to Jackson Memorial or Baylor?"

"You'd better come to *Baylor*," Jada said. "Dr. Davi has privileges there. I told you I ran into her a few weeks ago."

"But I'm so used to being on C3," he kidded. "I'm not trying to get used to some *substandard* hospital."

"Our cardiac wing is as state-of-the-art as theirs," Jada said with a frown. "Jackson ain't got nothing on us!"

"Why you getting defensive?" Evan asked, grinning.

"I'm just saying. Plus our cafeteria has way better food."

When they rounded the next corner, and their home was in sight, they noticed a vehicle they didn't recognize parked out front. As they drew nearer, they saw a stranger walking away from their door.

"Are you expecting someone?" Evan asked.

Jada shook her head. "No. I don't know who that is."

They made it home just as the stranger was approaching her car. She looked their way and smiled.

"Oh, I just rang your doorbell. Thought I'd missed you."

Jada and Evan looked at each other, still confused. Their visitor was middle aged with blonde hair that was starting to gray. Her eyes had a beautiful light green hue.

"I'm Sharon Bingham," she said, and recognition dawned in Evan and Jada's eyes. "I received the invitation to your wedding," she went on. "But I didn't want to meet you there. That day is all about the bride. I didn't want to take any shine away from her." She looked Jada up and down and smiled. "You are very beautiful. I'm sure you looked amazing in your dress."

Jada was momentarily speechless. "Thank you," she managed.

The woman turned back to Evan and watched him for a few moments. Gradually her attention settled on his chest, which rose and fell at a quickened pace due to their run. The woman's expression became melancholic as she stared at him. Her hand rose slowly. She caught herself before she made contact. She met his eyes again.

"Oh, I'm sorry. I didn't meant to..." Her eyes rolled down to his chest again. "Can I... Do you mind?"

Evan shook his head. "No, I don't mind." His expression was as heartfelt as hers.

She reached again, touching his chest tentatively with her fingers. She then flattened her palm. Her eyes slipped closed and she sighed. Tears spilled from both of her closed lids. When she opened her eyes, her beautiful green irises continued to gleam in a pool of tears.

"Cayden would've been 26 this month," she revealed. "There's not a day that goes by when I don't think about him."

Her eyes and hand were still on Evan's chest. The steady beating beneath her palm reverberated through her fingers, up her arm. Her tears continued to fall.

"Last night," she said, "I found an old shoebox in the closet. I had forgotten what was in it. It was..." She smiled. "It was a collection of old greeting cards I put away years ago – from Cayden. They were for Mother's Day, my birthdays. When he got older, he'd give me and my husband cards for our anniversary. It was... He was such a sweet kid. I..." She shuddered. Her smile faltered, but when she looked into Evan's eyes, it returned. "I'm glad he lives on through you."

Evan heard Jada sniffling by his side. Overcome with emotions, he began to cry too. He reached and pulled the woman into his embrace. He held her tightly as she rested her head on his chest and listened to his heartbeats. The neighborhood came to a standstill as they held and comforted each other, and the auburn sun continued to dip in the western sky.

KEITH THOMAS WALKER

ABOUT THE AUTHOR

Keith Thomas Walker, known as the Master of Romantic Suspense and Urban Fiction, is the author of more than two dozen novels, including *Fixin' Tyrone, Life After, The Realest Ever,* the *Backslide* series, the *Brick House* series and the *Finley High* series. Keith's books transcend all genres. He has published romance, urban fiction, mystery/thriller, teen/young adult, Christian, poetry and erotica. Originally from Fort Worth, he is a graduate of Texas Wesleyan University. Keith has won numerous awards in the categories of "Best Male Author," "Best Romance," "Best Urban Fiction," "Best Young Adult Romance," "Best Duo," "Book of the Year," and "Author of the Year," from several book clubs and organizations. Visit him at www.keithwalkerbooks.com.